THE
MENTOR

RITA CARLA FRANCESCA MONTICELLI

THE MENTOR

TRANSLATED BY AARON MAINES

amazon crossing

Previously published as *Il mentore* by the author via the Kindle Direct Publishing Platform in Italy in 2014. Translated from Italian by Aaron Maines. First published in English by AmazonCrossing in 2015.

Published by AmazonCrossing, Seattle

www.apub.com

Amazon, the Amazon logo, and AmazonCrossing are trademarks of Amazon.com, Inc., or its affiliates.

ISBN-13: 9781503947375
ISBN-10: 1503947378

Cover design by Scott Barrie

Printed in the United States of America

NOTE FROM THE AUTHOR

Although I included real and accurate information about the organization of police forces in London, I nevertheless took full artistic license concerning professional positions of numerous employees, as well as the logistics and procedures utilized by the Forensic Science Service Laboratory (an investigative unit of London's Metropolitan Police Service, the police department headquartered in New Scotland Yard) in order to better adapt them to the plot.

CHAPTER 1

1994

A jet of my mother's blood struck me in the face. She was clutching her neck, staring at me with imploring eyes. She tried to speak, but when she opened her mouth, little more than a gurgling sound came out.

I was standing next to her, petrified.

As much as she tried to stop it, blood ran between her fingers, staining the sky-blue bedcovers. The blood had created a dark, threatening stain on the bed that was constantly expanding.

I didn't understand.

She continued to wave her other hand fitfully. She kept pointing down.

When I'd first heard the shouting in the living room, I had run to my parents' bedroom and hidden beneath their bed. A few minutes later, someone came in. I recognized my mother's feet, but she wasn't alone. A man whispered to her, warning her to behave. If she did everything they wanted her to do, they wouldn't kill her.

I heard my mother whimpering.

Then there was a dull thud on the bed, and my mother's feet disappeared from view.

"Good, that's good," said the stranger. After that, I didn't see his feet anymore either.

I heard her shout and cry while the bed started moving the way it did when my brother jumped around on it to scare me, knowing that I was hiding underneath.

That movement went on for a little while, then it stopped.

The man released a deep sigh. "Did you like that? Tell the truth." I could hear the breathlessness in his voice.

My mother said nothing.

"Tell me you liked it, bitch!"

"I . . . liked it," she murmured at last.

Coarse laughter, then a sharp cry. After that, nothing but silence.

The man left the bedroom, and that's when I decided to leave my hiding place.

"Did you hurt yourself, Mama?"

I could feel my eyes fill with tears. I wanted to run into her arms and hug her, but I was afraid of all that blood.

Her body trembled. Once, twice, three times. Then her arm stopped moving and fell down to her side. Her eyes were empty, staring at nothing.

My teeth started chattering. I couldn't stop them. Shaking, I walked to the door and looked out into the hallway. Paul was lying on the floor, his face in the carpet. He wasn't moving either. There were bloodstains on the back of his pajama shirt.

For a moment I considered going out to shake him awake, but deep inside I knew that he couldn't help me anymore.

My father started screaming, and I turned toward the living room.

"No . . . please . . . !"

"No, please!" said a man. It was a new voice, different from the man in the bedroom. He was mimicking my father in a singsong tone. "Is that the best you can come up with?"

"I'll give you whatever you want; just leave my family alone," my father's voice cried out again.

I heard loud laughter, which stopped almost as quickly as it had started.

As if dragged forward by an inescapable force, I slowly walked, one foot after the next, toward the living room. When I reached the entry, I saw three men standing with their backs to me. They were tall, dressed in black. I immediately recognized the sneakers of the man who had killed my mother.

I felt light-headed, short of breath. I backed up immediately, hiding behind the half-closed door. But I couldn't bring myself to leave. I wanted to understand.

One of the strangers moved, allowing me to see my father. He was tied to a chair, one of the nice ones my mother never let me put my feet on. Blood was everywhere.

"Where is the safe?" asked one of the three. His voice seemed gentle, tender.

My father shook his head. "There's no safe—I swear to God!"

He'd barely finished the sentence before the man grabbed a bottle from the table and smashed him in the face with it. The glass shattered, sprinkling shards everywhere, and wine gushed out over my father's shirt.

"Don't lie to me!" shouted the voice. It didn't sound as nice now. "I know goddamned well you have a safe. Tell me where it is, and open it!"

"I swear I don't have a safe," said my father, begging. Blood ran from a gash on his head, and from another cut at the corner of his mouth.

The third man pointed a pistol at his temple. "Let's just kill this guy."

"Slow down. We need him alive. Otherwise, how d'you think we're gonna get that fucking safe open?"

The third man's face twisted into a grimace. He took the pistol away from my father's head and aimed it lower.

There was a gunshot, followed by more screams.

"Oh yeah? Now you're screaming, huh?" the third man said. "If you don't tell me where that safe is, I'll shoot your other foot too."

A fourth man walked in from the kitchen. "I have a better idea," he said. He was tall, and there was fire in his eyes. He was carrying an enormous knife in one hand. "I wanted to try this out on his wife, then on his son, but seeing as somebody had the brilliant idea of killing them without asking my permission . . ." He cast a disgusted look at the other three, all of whom moved away. There was an air about him, and he seemed like the leader of the gang, even though he was little more than a boy.

My father was frozen, waiting for his torturer to make his move.

"I'll just have to cut off this son of a bitch's fingers one by one until he tells me where the jewelry is."

For a fleeting moment I thought I saw a look of relief cross my father's face. At the time I didn't understand, but now I think he was thinking of me. My father must have realized they hadn't mentioned me, that maybe I was still alive. Maybe they didn't even know I existed.

"I'm not lying to you," said my father, speaking now with deliberate firmness. "I don't own a single piece of valuable jewelry. My wife has a few things in our room." He nodded toward the bedroom. "But they're not worth much. I'm just a regular guy with a regular job. You've got the wrong person."

"Shut your fucking mouth!" ordered the leader. "I know full goddamned well who you are, and if you really don't have anything valuable here, well, we'll find out soon enough!"

He motioned to the man next to him with one hand. The others went over to my father and grabbed his right wrist. They placed his

4

hand on the table next to the chair and pulled his pinkie finger out, forcing him to close the other fingers into a fist.

"No, please, you're making a mistake!"

The leader raised the knife over his head, then brought it down. There was a dull sound as the knife chopped through bone and stuck into the wood tabletop, but it was drowned out by cries of pain.

I never imagined my father was capable of making those sounds.

I backed up, a constricting feeling clutching my chest.

"I swear to God!" my father cried out.

I recognized the sound that came next, even though I couldn't see what was happening. I ran away, back into my parents' bedroom. My mother was still there, her eyes wide open, her body covered with blood. I didn't want to look at her, so I turned off the light before sliding under the bed again.

There were more screams from my father. They kept coming, unending. They continued for a long time—I don't know how long. I put my fingers in my ears and pushed as hard as I could until I couldn't hear anything anymore.

I stayed where I was, curled up in the darkness. Without realizing it, I slipped into a peaceful sleep, dreaming I was still in my bed and that all the horror was nothing more than a nightmare, that my mother would come and wake me and tell me to get ready for school.

But when I awoke I was still there, curled up on the rug beneath the bed, my hands aching from pressing them against my ears. When I uncovered my ears and listened, no sound came to meet them. Silence. Only the sound of the wind whistling through an open window. I opened my eyes. There was light. It was morning. Swirls of dust spun in front of me, illuminated by rays of sunlight. I sneezed.

There was a dull thud, and the wind stopped whistling.

"Goddamn it!" exclaimed a man's voice, authoritative. "Be careful, or you'll contaminate the scene."

Then footsteps came down the hall, followed by the clicking noise of a camera and the high-pitched whine of a flash recharging.

"Maybe the wind blew a window closed," suggested another male voice. This one sounded younger. "I'll go take a look."

Footsteps drew closer until I saw a pair of black shoes walk into the bedroom.

A sigh. "Fuck me," mumbled the new arrival. Then, speaking out loud, he added, "There's another victim in here!"

Another click with the camera. The man stooped lower. I could see his knees. He put something that looked like a ruler on the floor and then took another picture.

He seemed about to get back up again, but suddenly he stopped. He pointed his little flashlight at the floor and moved it around slowly, as if he was following something. My eyes were burning and my nose was running. I couldn't help myself. I sneezed again.

His face appeared immediately underneath the bed. The flashlight was in my eyes, blinding me. "Jesus Christ!" He turned off the light. I could see again. "Hey, sweetheart, are you okay?"

I stared at him, uncertain. Part of me wanted to respond to the tender, kind tone of his voice, but something held me back. A sense of mistrust, a sense of fear.

"Chief!" yelled the man, turning toward the door. "There's a little girl down here. She's alive! Call the paramedics." Then his face appeared back under the bed. "What's your name?"

I moved my lips, but no sound came out.

The man pointed his flashlight at a metal badge he wore on a cord around his neck. "I'm with the police. You don't have to be afraid. Come on, I'll bring you out of here." He stretched out his hand toward me. "My name is Eric. What's your name?"

I held out both arms to him. There was something reassuring in the sound of his voice. Or maybe it was his name. All I knew was that I wanted to get out of there, and he was going to help me.

Eric dropped the flashlight and took my hands in his. "Promise me you'll keep your eyes closed until I tell you it's all right to open them, okay?"

I nodded and did as he told.

I felt myself being pulled out from under the bed, then picked up and held. I wrapped my arms around his neck and buried my head in his chest. I could feel the heat coming from his body as he took long, quick steps through the house.

"Christ, a little girl . . ." said a woman's voice.

"Is the ambulance outside?" asked Eric.

"Yes. Take her there," said the authoritative voice I'd heard earlier.

We started moving again, and I held on with all my strength. I could smell chemicals in the fabric of his shirt, but it wasn't unpleasant. A calm started to come over me. His hand caressed my head tenderly, and each time he touched me I felt a little more protected, a little safer.

Finally I could feel the wind blowing my nightshirt and sense sunlight on my arms.

"Okay, you can open your eyes now."

I lifted up my head and opened them just a crack. The sunlight was strong, too strong, and I had to lift one hand to my face to shield my eyes. Then, little by little, I got used to it. I could see clearly the man who was holding me.

Eric smiled. It seemed like the most beautiful smile in the world—larger than his mouth. It was his whole face that smiled, even his eyes, which were a deep blue like the sea.

"Now will you tell me your name?" he asked.

I could feel my lips moving.

"Mina."

CHAPTER 2
TWENTY YEARS LATER

When Miriam Leroux hit the table hard with her hands, the man winced. She leaned in so close that their heads almost touched. A curl of chestnut-brown hair slid across her face. "We know it was you," she whispered. "And we can prove it. You're going to rot in jail for the rest of your life."

"There's no way you have any proof!" the suspect burst out.

She stood back up straight. "Oh no? Why not?"

"Because . . ." The suspect paused for a moment. "Because I'm innocent."

Detective Leroux started laughing. "Did you hear that? He says he's innocent," she said, and turned to Eric with a smile on her face.

Eric hadn't said a word during the entire interrogation. He'd stood there, impassive, while his colleague worked the suspect over. They'd refined their approach over time. He, head of the scientific investigations department, stood to one side, paging through a file and looking at them from time to time, apparently disinterested. The only signs he gave were occasional nods; then he'd smile faintly and go back to reading his file. Sometimes he might frown in faint annoyance and shake his head a little.

"We have proof that it was you, Johnson. This time you're finished." Miriam was serious again.

The suspect seemed a little disoriented. Perhaps because he'd been sure he hadn't left any proof of his involvement in the crime? Eric smiled to himself.

They'd been following this man for months. In every homicide that resembled an execution, his name came up. There was a suspicion that he was a hired assassin. He'd been seen near the victims' houses prior to the actual crimes, and Eric and Miriam were convinced it was no coincidence. He was a killer, but they couldn't establish a motive, so they had to base the investigation entirely on physical proof.

In each case they'd found the murder weapon: a gun, abandoned at the scene of the crime. The serial numbers were always removed, and ballistics had nothing to add. There were never any fingerprints on the guns, or anywhere else at the crime scene. The door locks were always intact. Everything pointed to a suicide, except for the fact that the same thing had happened twelve different times. Twelve people had taken their own lives at home, each using an untraceable firearm. Not one of them left behind a suicide note or displayed warning signs that they were about to take their own lives. Each victim had a number of known enemies, although it was impossible to connect any of them with the deaths. Alibis were ironclad and abundant.

A killer for hire. It hadn't taken long for the detective who ran the scientific investigations department and his young colleague of the Scotland Yard investigative team who was handling the twelve cases to arrive at this conclusion. With this theory in mind, gathering evidence from various video cameras located around the victims' homes, they'd identified Damien Johnson—an ex-soldier on leave who worked as a private security guard—in film from ten of the twelve cases. Digging into Johnson, they discovered he appeared to live beyond his modest means.

Johnson's sunken eyeballs stared out at Miriam, challenging her. "You don't have any proof," he said calmly, his thin face contracting slightly. "And this little game of good cop, bad cop won't work with me. I came here of my own free will, but I don't have to stay here unless you have a formal charge to bring against me."

Miriam kept watching him, an expression of detached curiosity on her face.

"Otherwise, you're going to be hearing from my lawyer," he added.

Without lifting his eyes from the folder, Eric took out a picture and put it on the table in front of Johnson. The man froze. "What's that supposed to be?" he asked.

"Those are your fingerprints," said Eric, finally breaking his long silence. "We found them on the murder weapon."

The suspect seemed to stop breathing for a moment. Then he shook his head. "That's a trick!" he shouted, shoving the photograph away. "Those aren't my fingerprints on a murder weapon."

"Oh no?" Eric stared into the man's eyes. "How come? Because you wore gloves?"

Johnson smiled again. "You keep bluffing. You don't have a thing."

"So if I test your right hand for gunpowder residue, it will come back negative, right?"

Johnson struggled to hold back a grimace. He seemed to think about that.

Eric knew perfectly well what was causing the suspect's change in behavior. The day before, Johnson had fired a shot into the air to scare off some wild dogs—they had been foraging near a mansion he was keeping an eye on for work. He'd reported the event to the company he worked for in order to justify the missing bullet. The test would come back positive in any case, and that was precisely what Eric and Miriam were counting on, even though there was almost no chance the residue would be compatible with the bullets they'd recovered from the scene of the crime. Johnson wasn't a criminologist, though, and if they got a confession, they might not even have to go to trial.

"I use guns every day for work," said Johnson, closing his eyes for a moment. Every inch of his body was struggling to project a calm he certainly didn't possess.

"Ah!" exclaimed Miriam, making no attempt to hide her sarcasm.

Eric motioned to her with one outspread hand. He was careful to appear calm, like someone who had everything under control. He knew that this would only make suspects more nervous, especially if they were guilty. And Johnson was undoubtedly guilty. He had escaped punishment too many times for lack of proof, but this time it was going to be different. With just a little push, they'd be able to lock him up. The fact that he'd just used his gun on the job was exactly the kind of opportunity they'd been waiting for to act.

"We have your prints on the gun. And as far as I understand, the residue tests on the gunpowder will come back positive." He glanced at the suspect, letting a complacent smile creep across his face. "You were seen near the victim's house the day before the murder. Maybe you were going over the final details of your plan?"

"My fingerprints aren't on that gun," said Johnson, looking his accuser in the eye.

"No? Are you sure?"

"There. Are. No. Fingerprints." The suspect pronounced his words carefully, one by one.

In truth, he was right, because Johnson had undoubtedly worn gloves. Or at least there hadn't been any fingerprints when they found the murder weapon at the scene. But there were fingerprints on it now. Because of the kind of work Johnson was doing, his fingerprints were registered in IDENT1, the digital British fingerprint database, so that he could be ruled out of any crimes that occurred in the places he was charged with keeping under surveillance. They were also registered in the military database, but fortunately they hadn't needed to go that far in order to obtain them. If they'd accessed that database, their move would not have passed unnoticed. After they'd obtained the prints, it was easy for an expert like Eric Shaw to find a way to make them show up on the weapon.

Shaw had asked personally to handle the case, something he did whenever one came along that he cared about deeply. His subordinates preferred to stay out of his way when he was working a case, even though Eric suspected that some of them realized he tended to fiddle a little with the proof. But who could blame him? He was certain they were dealing with an assassin who'd committed multiple crimes, but they couldn't find a way to lock him up. Their suspect had been too careful, too skilled at hiding his involvement. Eric felt like it was his duty to do something. He couldn't just stand by and let it happen.

Too many times over the course of his career he'd found himself faced with cases that went unresolved due to lack of physical evidence. The development of increasingly sophisticated forensic investigation techniques and his position as chief of the department were just tools Eric used in order to guarantee he brought the highest number of criminals possible to justice. Sometimes he had to use methods that weren't entirely orthodox.

He'd never once regretted his actions.

He was so good that all the evidence he provided proved to be ironclad, even during the trials. But his ability to invent evidence where there hadn't been any had earned him a certain notoriety among criminals. People who wound up in his sights knew there was little chance of escape, and this had won the detective more than one death threat. Shaw wasn't worried. By the same token, plenty of minor criminals were more than happy to roll on a larger fish in the hopes that they'd get special treatment in return.

"Our tests say exactly the opposite," Eric continued, pointing to the photograph in front of the suspect. "We found fingerprints on the murder weapon, and they are yours beyond a shadow of a doubt." He cleared his throat. "Maybe you forgot to use gloves."

Johnson was about to say something, then stopped. Of course he'd been wearing gloves. Eric didn't doubt it for a minute, but it was pointless to hope the suspect would admit that during an interrogation. No matter what Shaw said, Johnson knew he was burned. Shaw could see resignation in the man's eyes.

"I know you're not so naïve that you wouldn't wear gloves, but let's suppose for a minute that the situation got a little out of hand." Eric tapped his pen on the table. "It's a bright, sunny day, almost like summer outside. You know you can't walk around wearing gloves. You'd draw attention to yourself. Somehow you got into the victim's house, maybe using an excuse. At a certain point you realized that something wasn't working, and you had to kill him immediately. Then you cleaned the pistol, but you missed a fingerprint on the base of the handle. It happens—even the best of us get sloppy." He concluded with a broad, satisfied smile.

"I want a lawyer," said the suspect, before closing his mouth. He appeared to have ended the conversation once and for all.

"You could confess. You'd save us all a lot of time," said Miriam, sitting down on the edge of the table. "Maybe your willingness to help could earn you a few rewards. Maybe it could keep you from winding up sharing a cell with some very unpleasant fellows. You know, a guy like you, so handsome . . . pretty, even . . . always attracts certain *interests*."

"I want a lawyer!" he insisted.

"Okay." The detective jumped off the table and nodded to Eric, who stood up as well.

They left the interrogation room and closed the door behind them.

"Well, I'd say that went reasonably well," said Miriam, smoothing her shirt. "I think his lawyer will advise him to confess. That way we won't even have to bother with an obnoxious trial."

"I hope so," said Eric, smiling.

Miriam raised her palm and they high-fived—the way they had ever since she was a young girl.

The door to the next room opened. Martin Stern, an agent with the scientific investigations unit, walked out. He was accompanied by his young colleague, Adele Pennington. As soon as Eric saw her, he tensed up. He knew they'd had an audience looking on from the observation room, but he had no idea she was the one watching them.

"You were great in there, boss," Stern said with the enthusiasm of a little dog excited to see his master. Eric couldn't stand this sort of behavior, and in response he frequently punished Stern with the most unpleasant tasks to handle. His colleague never complained, though—instead he merely went about his business.

Adele, on the other hand, gave Eric a slight smile and a nod of approval, then spun on her heels and headed down the corridor.

"Hey, where are you going?" said Martin. "Wait for me."

"The show's over," said Adele. She stopped for a moment and gave her boss a serious look, her eyes darting back and forth between Shaw and Stern. "We've got work to do. Instead of hanging around here, you should come too," she said, then continued down the corridor toward the elevator.

Stern flared. For months Eric had watched as Stern tried everything he could to make friends with Pennington, and as she completely snubbed him in return. To be honest, Adele behaved that way with everybody. The only one she was polite to, or at least seemed to try to be polite to, was Eric, her boss. But even then she never stepped over the line. She spoke her mind with everyone, never worrying for a moment what their reactions might be, especially when it came to criticizing them for not working hard enough. At the same time, she was putting a wall up between herself and her colleagues in order to keep them from getting too close to her. This made her the object of unconcealed hatred among her female coworkers, while the men—as could be expected—were crazy about her.

Not even Eric, three months away from his fiftieth birthday and twenty-two years her senior, was immune to her attractions. He was old enough to be her father, and knowing this made him uncomfortable, especially since he had the strong sensation that she was aware of how he felt and that it disgusted her. She had every right to be disgusted. In the end, he was an *old man*.

Eric's eyes met Stern's. "Your colleague is right," he said, growing serious. He enjoyed torturing Stern, perhaps more than he should. The more Stern tried to endear himself to Eric, the more Eric underlined his shortcomings.

"Oh . . . yeah, of course. Right, boss," said Stern, practically saluting. "I'll get back to work right away!" He ran down the corridor. "Adele, sweetheart, wait up. Hold the door, would you?" But before he could reach the elevator, Adele waved to him with one hand and let the doors close in his face.

Eric and Miriam started laughing. "Pennington's just sugar and spice and everything nice, isn't she?" said Leroux.

Eric smiled. "You can say that again."

"Our fearless leader strikes again!" exclaimed Jane Hall, smiling as she stormed into Eric's office. Hall was Eric's second in command.

From behind his desk, he shot her a questioning look, lifting his eyes slightly from the computer screen.

"You haven't heard?" Jane flopped down in a chair and put her feet up on the table.

Eric grabbed a file pinned beneath one of Jane's shoes, managing to pull it away as she crossed her legs. "Heard what?" he asked, smoothing the crumpled paperwork with one hand.

Rita Carla Francesca Monticelli

"Johnson confessed. Right now he's working out a deal with the crown prosecutor. He's willing to give up the name of his client in exchange for a reduced sentence. Unfortunately, we can only connect him directly to the latest murder. We don't have any proof for the others, save the fact that the killings occurred with the same modus operandi and that he was seen around the other victims' houses. Both interesting clues. Maybe we can squeeze a little more information out of him with the threat of being charged with the other crimes as well."

Jane spoke all in a rush, the way she usually did. It was an approach that disoriented her interlocutors, especially when they were suspects or when she was speaking during trial depositions. On more than one occasion, it had allowed her to help prosecutors send a fair number of criminals to prison. She'd worked for the Forensic Science Service Laboratory, Scotland Yard's scientific investigations unit, for over fifteen years and was one of the most talented criminologists on Eric's staff. He trusted her completely, even though he felt that sometimes she tended to be a little too optimistic.

"Johnson seemed pretty savvy," he said, dropping the file in a drawer. Eric took one last glance at the computer screen, then leaned back in his chair. He'd finish filing his report later. "If he figures out that our evidence is merely circumstantial and wouldn't hold up in court, or if he learns that it shouldn't even be allowed, then he'll start denying everything. He'll negotiate a deal for the last murder and manage to do as little jail time as possible."

Even though they'd caught him, the fact that they couldn't tie Johnson to the other murders, which Eric was sure he was responsible for, left a bitter taste in his mouth. It wasn't so much because the killer would get away—in any case, he'd spend quite a while behind bars—but rather because all those other crimes would go unpunished. There were eleven cases in London alone; nailing Johnson would only answer for one dead body.

Despite often resorting to questionable methods and risking his reputation and career to see guilty parties punished, Eric knew that he simply wouldn't be able to catch everyone. In truth, he didn't care one whit about the shady tactics he employed. He didn't have much to lose. His personal life was a disaster. His total, unyielding focus on work had distanced him from his family to the point that, one fine day, his wife had taken their only son, Brian, and left him for good. That was nine years ago, but Eric still hadn't gotten over it. To cope, he'd thrown himself deeper into his work. Night and day bled together—sometimes he'd find himself working cases on Saturdays and Sundays. He spent less and less time at home, and when he returned he mostly sat around thinking about what he had left undone. He often slept in the office, where he always kept a clean change of clothing in case the need arose.

The murders staged to look like suicides had been gnawing at him for months, and even now, after they'd finally gotten their man, he still didn't feel satisfied. It was a minor victory, and really not much of one compared to the fact that plenty of criminals were still free walking the streets. He knew he'd done the best he could, overcoming every limit he'd imposed on himself in order to finally trap Johnson. But it hadn't been enough.

"Come on, don't make that face." Jane shrugged. "We'll double our efforts. We'll open the older cases back up and work twice as hard to unravel them. We'll find something. There's no such thing as a perfect killer. If we rifle through eleven cases, I'm sure we'll find another mistake somewhere. And if we can connect him to at least one other murder, demonstrate the repeated use of a consolidated pattern, I'm sure we'll be able to bring him to trial for the other murders too."

She always saw the positive side of things. That was one of the reasons Eric, as soon as he'd been promoted to head of the scientific investigations department, had selected Jane as his second in command. She was a little like a guardian angel, someone who dragged him back up into reality when depression threatened to gain the upper hand. Jane had been happy to accept the role, and she pulled it off with an almost maternal flair.

He'd met her only after his separation, and she'd been by his side during the agonizing divorce. She'd never seen the old Shaw in action, the meticulous agent who, enamored with forensics, relied on the truthfulness of his evidence as the foundation for everything else. She'd only interacted with his subsequent disillusioned doppelgänger.

They'd never spoken openly about his methods, but Eric was certain she knew. She was too careful and aware to miss certain details, but she'd never mentioned it to him. He couldn't say whether she did this to protect him, or merely to protect herself. But even if the former were her only motive, it was still the right way to act. Making her an accomplice would have made him feel even pettier than he already did.

A woman wearing a white shirt passed by the glass door to his office. Adele. Eric thought he caught a quick look of disapproval shot in his direction.

Maybe it was just his mind playing tricks on him.

He felt Jane's hand tighten on his shoulder, dragging him back to the present. He'd been so lost in his thoughts that he hadn't realized she'd stood up and walked over to where he was sitting at his desk. "If you keep on like this, sooner or later she'll pick up on it," she said with an allusive grimace.

Eric pretended to be shocked by what she was saying, but he knew he wasn't very convincing.

Ever since Pennington had joined his team a little over six months ago, he'd felt overwhelmed by emotions he didn't fully understand. He kept telling himself he was just a lascivious old man ogling young women, and he reproached himself for his own feelings. He convinced himself that it was simply a minor midlife crisis, and that it would all blow over soon enough. But it wasn't blowing over, and he'd begun to think that maybe he wasn't so old after all. He looked good for a forty-nine-year-old. These were a man's best years, and he might easily appear attractive to a young, twenty-seven-year-old woman.

He shook his head at this thought. Who was he trying to fool?

Jane started laughing. For a moment he was afraid he'd said something out loud, but the laughter was just Jane's way of letting her colleague know she knew him all too well.

Jane would have made the perfect companion for him. He needed someone capable of fending off his obsession for his work, and Jane was that. She was also married, happily. He pushed the thought from his head. She wasn't his type anyway . . . or was she? That was just another excuse. The truth was he didn't want a challenging relationship, one he'd risk fucking up the way he'd fucked up his marriage. It was much easier to spend time fantasizing about a young, unobtainable colleague than it was to actually get out there and start dating again.

Suddenly his cell phone rang. A second later Jane's cell phone rang too.

The stench of death hung heavy in the room. A cloud of flies buzzed around, feeding off the mutilated body.

The landlord had been the first one to discover the body after he had decided to use his keys to open the door. He hadn't seen his tenant, Nicholas Thompson, for a number of days. Thompson had missed his rent, and a few of his neighbors had complained about the foul stink wafting from his apartment.

Until then, Thompson had always been an excellent tenant. The landlord never had a single reason to complain about him. In fact, he found the man funny and personable, so these developments troubled him. He was quick to worry that something had happened to him. But when the landlord had opened the front door, he certainly wasn't expecting to find himself face to face with a horrifying spectacle.

At first he hadn't really understood what he was looking at. He'd thought it was some sort of mannequin. He'd hoped it was someone's idea of a bad joke. After turning on the light, there was no room for doubt. One look was enough to recognize the tenant, even despite all the blood surrounding the corpse.

Who could have done such a thing to poor Nick?

As far as the landlord knew, he was an honest, hardworking man. Nick had retired only a few months earlier, and just a couple of weeks ago he had confided to the landlord that he couldn't wait for August to arrive, because his son had promised to bring his family to visit. He had seemed truly moved and excited by the idea of that reunion.

Now it was all over.

In truth, the landlord didn't know much about the man. He'd heard stories about Nick's past, a few arrests for thievery when he was younger, but nothing serious. He seemed to have gotten his head on straight. He'd been living there for over ten years, and every day Nick had left early in the morning to head for work.

Thinking about all this, the landlord realized that he'd heard a phone ringing on more than one occasion, but he hadn't been sure it was Nick's. He lived next door, but the walls in the building were so thin and insubstantial that everyone could hear what was going on.

He didn't have any trouble telling the police lady precisely that.

"Thank you," said Miriam. "We'll be in touch if we need additional information." She handed him a business card. "Call me at this number here if anything else should come up." Then she turned around and waved at the scientific investigations team, who were just now walking into the room.

"Hey," said Jane, her lips tightening. "Let me guess . . . Judging by the stink, I'd say at least a week."

"Let's make that ten days," said the investigations doctor, Richard Dawson. He was leaning over the corpse, examining it.

Eric shouldered past his colleague and the other agents so that he could take a close look at the crime scene. After solving the Johnson case, he'd hoped to relax a little, at least for the rest of the day. But life had other plans.

"Another honest citizen massacred without any clear motivation, I imagine," said Eric, casting an inquisitive look in Miriam's direction.

At that very moment Adele stepped past him, brushing against his arm. She had a look of concentration on her face. She didn't say hello to anyone in the room but simply started taking photographs.

"A gunshot to the neck, which lacerated his carotid artery," said Dr. Dawson, addressing no one in particular. "Another to the groin. No sign of exit wounds. At first glance I'd say he died from loss of blood almost immediately."

"Nicholas Thompson, Nick, a sixty-five-year-old repeat offender who appears to have kept himself out of trouble for at least the last fifteen years," said Miriam, providing a quick summary of the case.

Even though she was the detective assigned to the investigation, when she worked with Shaw she shared all the data she had with him, and they generally tried to resolve the crime by working together. The team was a well-assorted and often-winning combination of individuals. "No one heard the shots, and given that the walls aren't exactly soundproof," Miriam added, pointing to the walls on either side, "I'm guessing the gun had a silencer."

The camera flash illuminated the room, forcing Eric to blink and making his head ache. He had slept little the night before and could already sense that he'd be going to bed later than he'd hoped tonight too. "An execution. There's a lot of that going around lately," he said drily.

"Yes, it certainly looks like one," said Miriam. She was standing alongside him, watching Jane and Adele work.

"Whoever carried it out, however, wanted to leave a very specific message." Eric stepped in close to the corpse. "If they'd merely wanted to kill him, a shot to the head would have been enough. But one in the neck and another in the groin . . . hmm . . . Do we know if he was ever involved in any sex crimes?"

"He was a thief who specialized in apartments," Miriam said, reading the dossier on her smartphone. "No formal accusations for sex crimes. Seems like he wasn't the violent type." She shrugged. "Of course, we don't know about additional crimes he was never charged with."

Eric looked over Thompson's body, thinking to himself. There was something familiar about the man splayed out on the floor, but he couldn't quite figure out what. It was a sensation more than anything else. In truth, he felt so completely tired that his sensations could have meant everything or nothing. He smiled, resigned. "Let's cover every inch of this place," he said loudly to his entire team. "Was the door forced?" he asked Miriam.

She shook her head, slipping the cell phone back into her pocket. "It was locked. No signs of forced entry. There's no key either. The landlord opened it with his key, then called us immediately."

Turning to the entrance, which opened directly into the living room of the little apartment, Eric tried to reconstruct the scene. "He knew his assassin, or at least was willing to let him in. He didn't think he was in danger." He imagined Thompson opening the door and letting an undefined figure enter. "But whoever he let in aimed a pistol at him, shooting him first in the throat so that he couldn't cry out for help, then in the groin. The victim falls on the floor and quickly dies from loss of blood. The killer may have stayed here to watch him die." The unfocused figure Eric had in his mind was now standing right alongside him. "Then he took the keys, closed the door carefully, and took off."

"It was personal," murmured Miriam, putting her hands on her hips. She curled her lips and blew a strand of hair away from one side of her face.

"We'll do our best here," Eric said as his eyes focused on the crime scene again. "But I need you to dig into this guy's life, because I'm certain we'll find whoever's responsible for his death in there somewhere."

FROM MINA'S BLOG

It's funny how, when you're little, people seem bigger than they really are. To my eyes, as I was looking at his shoes from underneath the bed, that man seemed like a giant. But when I found myself facing him twenty years later, I realized just how short he really was.

As soon as he opened the door, the first thing that caught his attention was my neckline. Maybe because it was the closest thing to his eye level. I had unbuttoned my shirt precisely because I knew it would make things easier. Only after that did he raise his eyes to look me in the face.

I knew at once, from the way his face relaxed, how happy my presence made him. A young, beautiful girl at his door. I was undoubtedly a pleasant surprise.

I introduced myself, and just as I'd imagined, he didn't recognize my name. In fact, he let me in immediately so that we wouldn't have to talk standing there in the doorway. It was even easier than I'd thought it would be. I'd made up a credible story in order to justify my visit, but I didn't get a chance to use it. Maybe I'll get a chance later.

He told me to make myself at home and asked if I wanted some tea. He went to make a pot right away. I got the sense he didn't get a lot of visitors, because he seemed to want to do everything he could to keep me there as long as possible, just to have someone to talk to.

He started talking about the weather—one of those pointless conversations about how this summer was looking rainier than usual, and how melancholy that made him feel.

"Being British and hating the rain sounds like a singular punishment, don't you think?" he asked, laughing at his own joke. I laughed too. What a loveable little man.

Then he started going on about the different varieties of tea he was preparing, and how when he was younger he paid less attention to those details, how he'd been too absorbed by his frenetic life. He really liked it when I told him I'd heard of the various teas.

When we finally sat down at the table, facing one another, he looked at me closely for the first time. "Excuse me for asking, miss, but have we met before? I feel like I've seen you somewhere."

He'd never seen me before, but I know that I look a lot like my mother. When he killed her, she'd only been a few years older than I am right now.

"Not exactly," I said. "But you've had the pleasure of meeting my parents and my brother, even if only for a few hours."

The man squinted a little, as if he were trying to remember. I could see he was struggling with his memory. "I'm sorry, miss," he said, his mouth curling into a little frown, almost as if he was embarrassed. "I'm getting old now, and my memory isn't quite what it used to be. I had a few problems with drugs and alcohol when I was younger, and I have to admit that a lot of my memories from those years have turned hazy. Give me a little hint. When did I meet your family?"

I had set the package I brought with me in my lap. He couldn't see me slip my hand inside it and take its contents out beneath the table. "Twenty years ago," I said. "I was just seven. You didn't see me, but I saw you very well, and I never forget a face."

He seemed curious to hear what I was saying, but at the same time his expression darkened, as if somewhere in the back of his head unpleasant thoughts were starting to push their way up through his memories.

I smiled. "My father was thirty-four, my mother was thirty-one, and my brother was just nine years old."

Thompson's brow furrowed.

I stopped smiling, and the tone of my voice grew hard. "And the safe was upstairs."

The man's eyes turned enormous, and it seemed like some faint thread of recognition appeared there. His mouth dropped open. "Oh, fuck me," he whispered, standing up in a rush, knocking over the chair behind him.

I stood up as well, pointing the pistol with the long silencer straight at him. "Behave, Nick. Lie down on the floor." I started laughing. "You'll like it; you'll see."

CHAPTER 3

He yawned in front of the papers spread out across his desk, then checked the time on his computer screen. It was after nine already. Saturday night, and he had been working nonstop since eight that morning. After having pored over the Thompson murder scene, he began dusting off old cases together with Miriam, searching for leads. They hadn't found anything noteworthy. Nowadays all the information and proof collected in each case was archived in the Metropolitan Police's main server and was available for review with a click of the mouse, but the farther back you looked, the more fragmented and incomplete the data became. The process by which material evidence was transferred to digital storage continued nonstop, but it privileged the crimes people believed to be more important than others. Minor theft or charges that were brought and then later dropped, as often happened with sexual abuse charges, wound up at the bottom of the list. You had to go back to the old paper files, which were full of irrelevant information, yellowed photographs, and barely legible handwritten notes.

Eric took off his reading glasses and pressed two fingers into his forehead, as if to drive away the ache that had been twisting its way through his head for hours.

Maybe he should give up for tonight and get a good night's sleep. He knew that he would have to make a superhuman effort tomorrow to prevent himself from coming back to the department. His body needed rest, but his mind couldn't stop turning over the details. He feared that if he loosened his grip, he'd be forced to come to terms with the way he was living and wind up spending another day off wallowing in memories and melancholy, full of self-pity—like he usually did on the weekends he spent without his kids. He would have loved to just go to bed, sleep all day Sunday, and wake up ready to go on Monday morning. Unfortunately, he could rarely stay asleep for more than seven hours, and so in any case he'd wind up watching the sun rise on yet another day in his useless existence.

And then he'd wind up back here, in Scotland Yard.

Eric turned off the computer and put on his jacket. Outside it was pouring rain against the window, and he had no idea where he'd put his umbrella. The St. James's Park station was just a short walk away, but he'd already be soaked by walking from the New Scotland Yard exit to the gate surrounding the building.

As Eric walked down the hallway, out of the corner of his eye he noticed a light on in one of the laboratories. He wasn't the only person putting in a late night. He peeked through the doorway and found someone wearing a white lab coat at a large table in the center of the room. She arranged sealed envelopes with one hand while checking a tablet, which she held in the other. Her back was turned, but he recognized her immediately all the same. Her graceful bearing and chestnut-brown hair with auburn highlights that glimmered in the bright ceiling lights were dead giveaways.

Eric stood still and watched her for a moment. Adele seemed unaware she had company. She worked in silence. Since he was headed home, he should at least say good-bye, maybe ask what she was still doing in the office. Anybody else would have, but Eric wasn't sure how to behave with her. For the moment he settled for watching her undisturbed, unknown to anyone, even her. That didn't happen often, and he didn't want to deprive himself of this dubious pleasure, even though he could feel there was something inherently wrong in doing so. Maybe he should just slip away silently, hoping she didn't realize he'd ever been there.

"Good evening, boss," she said. Her busy, matter-of-fact tone made him wince just a little. How long had she known he was standing there? "What are you doing here? Working late again today?" The way she said this made it sound like nothing more than the usual courteous work-place convo. But hearing Adele speak directly to him gave Eric a vague sense of excitation, mixed with a subtle feeling of panic.

It was as if he'd gone back to being a teenager, getting all excited when the most beautiful girl in school happened to wave to him by chance. He was her boss, for crying out loud!

"Yeah," was all he managed to say. "What are you up to?" That was right, he was the boss. "You should be at home. Your shift ended hours ago." He almost bit his own tongue. He never meant to let her know that he kept track of which shifts she was covering. Who knows what she might think?

"Jane had important plans tonight, so I offered to finish cataloguing this stuff for her. It wasn't like I had anything more important to do."

The indifference in her voice seemed to confirm his observation, but Eric still wasn't convinced. One thing was for sure: a girl like her would have a million things to do during the weekend, but giving your superior a helping hand never hurt. It might even wind up being useful.

When it came to work ethic, Jane had an excellent opinion of Adele, but she didn't feel the same way about her on a personal level. Jane considered the younger woman to be something of a robot, some-one who was disinterested in being friends with her colleagues and even considered herself superior to them. A nice gesture from Adele like this might improve Jane's opinion of her. Even in a worst-case scenario, it would make Jane feel a little beholden to Adele. This favor might even convince Jane to give the younger woman a little benefit of the doubt and suspend her judgment awhile longer.

In the meantime, Adele had taken off her lab coat and put on a purple leather jacket. Now she was searching for something in her purse, which seemed large enough to pass for luggage rather than a handbag. Clearly she was about to leave the building. Maybe he should wait for her, given that they were the last two left, but he couldn't be sure the gesture would be welcomed.

"Well . . . Have a good weekend," said Eric. Adele seemed to ignore him, busy pulling a small foldable umbrella out of her purse. Against his will, Eric turned and started walking away.

"Hold on, boss; wait for me!" she said. "I'm headed out too."

Eric was paralyzed as Adele emerged from the laboratory.

She closed the door behind her and walked right past him, overtaking him. Then she turned back to her boss and gave him an inquisitive look.

Realizing only then that she was waiting for him, Eric walked after her.

Adele reached the atrium and pressed the button for the elevator. Eric waited beside her, scrupulously careful not to stand too close.

She glanced at her cell phone for a moment, snorted, and then stuck it back in her jacket pocket. "Still no car," she said, staring distractedly at the elevator doors opening in front of them. "That damned mechanic promised it would be ready this morning. Now it looks like they're missing another piece, and it won't be ready until next week." She walked into the elevator, and Eric followed her. He had no idea what to say. "Tomorrow I'm going to have to borrow my sister-in-law's beater, and then I have to drive halfway across London. What a drag." It wasn't clear whether she was talking to Eric or to herself. She seemed intent on listening to the sound of her own voice.

Eric pushed the button for the ground floor, and the doors closed. Neither one said anything during the short trip down. Adele buttoned up her jacket, adjusted the purse over her shoulder, and got ready to open her umbrella.

When they reached the ground floor, she left the elevator without saying a word, walking quickly toward the exit. Eric did the same, but with less conviction, watching her walk ahead of him and feeling more depressed than ever. He'd just been given an opportunity to talk to the only woman who lit a spark in his heart, and he'd wasted it. He'd been unable to say anything more engaging than "Yeah" and "Have a nice weekend."

"I'm going to head out to Leicester Square and grab a bite to eat," she said.

Eric looked up and met her eyes. He was stunned. He thought she'd hurried off without a good-bye, but she was standing by the door, waiting for him.

"Will you keep me company?" added Adele once he was near. For the first time she looked him in the face when talking to him. She wasn't smiling. In fact, she didn't seem all that convinced of the offer she'd just made him. It was as if she'd asked only out of common courtesy—another favor that might prove useful to her in the future, just like with Jane.

Even though he was aware of how things stood between them, Eric felt a jolt of adrenaline course through his veins. For a moment he was short of breath.

Adele continued to look at him. In just a few seconds her expression turned from cordial to impatient. Maybe she was already regretting the question, now tired of waiting for an answer that still hadn't come. "So?" she asked.

Part of Eric was opposed to the way she addressed him, but at the same time he couldn't let such a terrific opportunity slip through his fingers. "Sure, why not?" He tried to say it as naturally as he could, but his voice came out practically choked with tension.

A slight smile appeared on Adele's lips. "Good." Then she headed out the door. Once outside, she paused and opened her umbrella. "Come on. I've got you covered," she added, looking up at it high overhead.

By the time they came out at Leicester Square station, the rain had stopped. During the ride and their transfer at Embankment station, Adele hadn't said a word. She checked her cell phone half a dozen times, apparently entertained by the messages she was answering, and smiled vaguely in his direction every once in a while.

The more time that went by, the more crestfallen Eric felt. How could he possibly aspire to a woman like this? She was undoubtedly chatting with her boyfriend, telling him she'd be late because she'd taken pity on her poor, ancient boss and now had to nanny him through dinner. He wished he could come up with a decent excuse and escape back home, but he had nothing.

They walked across the square and soon wound up in a little side street bustling with people. It was just like any other Saturday night. There were people of all ages and from all over the world, all ignoring the foul weather, wandering around as couples or in groups. The females were dressed to the nines, wearing thin, clingy clothing even though it was barely fifty degrees Fahrenheit out. They didn't care. Eric looked around and smiled. This unexpected landscape of laughter and happiness lifted his spirits almost immediately. He remembered when he too enjoyed blending in with the crowds. It wasn't so long ago, walking along with his wife and enjoying life in general.

Out of the corner of his eye he noticed that Adele was scrutinizing him.

They reached a pub, and as soon as they stepped inside, a young man ran over to Adele and gave her a big hug. Eric realized she was a regular here, because after the warm welcome they were ushered to a table instantly, almost by magic. He suspected that his companion had skipped ahead of a few reservations thanks to her friendship with one of the managers. Maybe she came here every Saturday; maybe there was always a table waiting for her.

He didn't know much about her. In fact, now that he thought about it, he knew nothing about her. She might as well be co-owner of the pub, and it might be possible that the young man worked for her. Maybe he was her cousin. He certainly hoped so, because given the way they said hello, they seemed on intimate terms. Watching them together had already made him a little jealous.

They ordered steaks, and after they'd enjoyed their first beer, Eric's mood improved even further. Adele seemed to be having fun and was more inclined to have an actual conversation. To tell the truth, they were just talking about work, but they didn't have anything else in common, and in any case it was nice to do so in an atmosphere other than their cold, impersonal office.

"Do you come here a lot?" he asked her.

"Often enough. It's a nice pub." Adele looked around. "The people who work here are really nice. They serve great food and the prices are even better." Her lips expanded into an enigmatic smile.

The alcohol was helping Eric feel a little more sure of himself, and he responded to that smile in a natural manner without a trace of guilt. He tossed back the last of his second pint and stood up. "All this liquid is starting to crank up the pressure," he said without thinking.

Adele burst out laughing. "Go ahead, boss. I won't hold you back."

When he got back from the bathroom, he saw that his empty glass had been replaced with another full mug. They'd finished eating, but evidently they hadn't finished drinking. He had no idea what time it was and wouldn't have cared even if he did. He hoped the night would keep going and going forever.

Adele lifted up her glass theatrically to salute him. "To his majesty!" she declared solemnly, then started laughing.

Eric accepted the toast and they clinked glasses. "God save the queen!" he replied, then guzzled his beer until his breath gave out. He felt a wave of heat hit him almost immediately. It wasn't the same beer they'd ordered earlier. It was much stronger, but he didn't mind the added punch. What he did care about was that Adele was having fun, and from the smile on her face, she seemed to be having plenty.

"Maybe you don't know this," he said, "but your colleagues don't like you very much." Wait, what? Had he really just said that? His mouth appeared to have disconnected completely from his brain.

She laughed, tilting her head into her right hand and plunging her fingers into her hair. With her other hand, she ran her fingers lightly around the edge of the beer glass.

Eric couldn't figure out whether she was amused more by what he'd said or by the way he'd said it. He realized he was a little drunk. No, that was wrong. He wasn't a little drunk; he was drunk, simply and completely. He hadn't gotten drunk in years and would undoubtedly have a raging headache tomorrow and regret every word that was coming out of his mouth—but what the hell? Maybe he wouldn't even remember what he'd said. Whatever the case, he felt incapable of stopping himself.

"I'm serious. Except for Stern, who's crazy about you . . ." He wondered why the heck he'd been so scared of talking to her just a few hours earlier. It was so easy now.

"Lord, that louse?" said Adele. She straightened her head and let an index finger slide down across her lips. "He'll do anything I say. You have no idea how useful that can be, really."

She really was every bit the bitch they all said she was, but instead of annoying him, it just made him laugh. For a moment it occurred to him that she might be saying equally unpleasant things about him to the others behind his own back, but he pushed the thought aside as quickly as he could. He didn't care about that now. Nothing mattered except the moment.

He finished his glass. When he put it back down on the table, his aim was inexplicably off, and it wound up in pieces on the floor, earning him a cheer from the rest of the pub.

"Okay, boss. Maybe we'd better step outside for some fresh air." Adele stood and took him by the arm, pulling him up too. But when Eric tried to stand, his head started spinning out of control, and he had to lean on the table to keep from falling over.

He found it harder and harder to keep track of what was happening around him, while his companion struggled to help him get back on his feet.

Fresh air, swollen with humidity that promised more rain to come, seemed to help pierce the fog that was muddying his thoughts.

Adele and the young man from the pub had him sit down on a low stone wall. He watched them chatting right in front of him. Every once in a while she reached out and touched his arm in an intimate manner. "Everything okay, boss?"

Eric nodded, trying to smile, but he immediately felt a wave of nausea and had to bend over to vomit. The other two grabbed him immediately to give a helping hand, keeping him from toppling over. After he'd liberated his stomach of what was left of his dinner, the nausea passed, along with most of his sense of disorientation.

"Are you sure you don't need any help?" asked the young man. Now that he could see him more clearly, Eric realized he must have been around thirty years old.

Adele handed Eric a tissue. She kept her other hand on his shoulder in a comforting gesture. "Thanks, but I think I can take care of him myself from here on out."

"Okay." The young man gave her a good-bye hug. "See you soon then."

"Count on it."

He winked at her and then headed back into the pub. Adele waved to him, then sat down on the wall alongside Eric.

Eric knew full well that under normal circumstances, he would have been incredibly embarrassed by what had just happened, but right now he couldn't feel it. Despite everything, he felt filled with a warm glow of well-being.

"Are you feeling better? I mean, seriously." She threw him an inquisitive look, the same he'd seen her use countless times before when she was concentrating on her work.

"Yes, seriously." The words came out of his mouth clearly, a sign that perhaps his brain and his vocal cords had reestablished their connection. "You guys seemed really close. He your boyfriend?" There we go. The connection worked, but data transmission was still a little sketchy.

Adele turned in the direction her friend had headed. He could barely make out the expression of affection mixed with melancholy cross her face. "He's my ex."

"Oh . . ." Fortunately Eric's brain didn't come up with anything inconvenient to say. "Were you guys really close?" Ah, there it was.

"We're divorced."

Those last words stunned him for a moment. They had something else in common. Up until now, it was the only thing he'd found.

"So young and already divorced . . ." He said this with a very sincere tone of sadness. He knew full well the repercussions something like that could have on a person's life. Eric reminisced for a moment about the way this woman had behaved ever since she'd arrived in their department, and he found himself understanding her a little better. Her standoffishness and the way she interacted with her colleagues might all have far simpler motives than the thousands of unpleasant suppositions that had crossed his mind.

"I'm old enough to have a failed marriage behind me, yes," she said, turning back to Eric. She seemed almost annoyed that he'd said she was too young, but her eyes told another story. The tale of a woman who was poking fun at her *elderly* boss.

"But you guys stayed on good terms," said Eric. "I wish I'd been able to do that with my ex."

"To be honest, we still love each other, but . . ."

He waited for her to finish, staring at her lips.

Adele hesitated a little longer, apparently enjoying keeping him in suspense. "The problem is . . . he's gay!" Then she laughed.

It wasn't much of a laugh. The divorce must have been an incredibly upsetting experience, although perhaps over time she'd gotten over it. Or maybe she was just really good at hiding her emotions. Even now that they were alone, with Eric's defenses lowered thanks to alcohol, Adele appeared to keep up the walls that separated her from the rest of the world, preventing anyone from getting too close to her.

She took out her cell phone for the umpteenth time. As soon as she touched the screen it lit up, casting a cold light onto her face. "You're too drunk to take the tube," she said, touching buttons on her screen. "I'm calling a cab."

Ten minutes later they were sitting in the backseat of a taxi. Eric intended to rest his head for a moment on the window, but he slipped into a deep sleep. Adele watched him, a little worried, while the car took off down Oxford Street. She was concerned he'd collapse from one moment to the next.

When the taxi driver took a right turn into Portman Street a little too quickly, she put her arms around her boss to hold him upright. The last thing she needed was for him to knock his head on something. Then she would have to take him to the emergency room, and the news that the most famous squad leader in the scientific investigations department of Scotland Yard had wound up at the hospital, too drunk to function, would make its way around London in a heartbeat. It would deal quite a blow to his reputation, and Adele didn't want to be the least bit responsible for that.

The car came to a brusque stop. She realized they'd already reached Dorset Street, right outside the building where she lived. She tried to shake Eric gently.

"Boss, this is my stop. Can you hear me?"

He mumbled something incomprehensible in response.

"I have to get out here. We have to tell the taxi driver where to take you, so that he can get you home," she said, raising her voice a little.

This time Eric didn't even try to respond. He'd fallen asleep again.

The taxi driver turned around and opened the little window that separated the front from the back of the car. "Hey, your buddy's good and drunk, isn't he?" There was a certain element of commiseration in his eyes. "I don't think the evening's gone quite as planned, has it?"

The man seemed to have developed very clear ideas about the two passengers in the back. Maybe he thought they were a classic pair: the boss with his young secretary. He'd invited her out for drinks in the hope of taking her to bed, and she'd accepted in the hope of getting a raise or a promotion, but things had gotten out of hand, and now all they'd have left were hangovers and hazy memories. The driver's laughter seemed to confirm that was his opinion of the events.

"Listen," said Adele, turning to face the taxi driver. "I'll give you twenty quid on top of the fare if you'll help me get him up to my place."

"Hmm," said the man, and nothing more. Maybe he was thinking this request didn't fit well with the story he'd imagined. Or maybe he just wanted to barter his way to a bigger bonus.

"Have you gotten any tickets lately, by any chance?" Adele asked. Perhaps there was another way they could work out a deal.

"What do you care?" replied the taxi driver, and not politely.

At this point Adele pulled out her badge and showed it to him. The driver's face turned serious, then melted into a timid smile. There was no doubt that if she checked the vehicle's paperwork she'd find something out of order. She wasn't a street cop, but this man didn't know that.

"Ah!" he exclaimed. "I don't want a thing, miss. I'm happy to give you a hand." The way he said it, it almost seemed true.

* * *

"Where are we going to put him?" asked the driver as soon as they were in Adele's apartment. "Wow! Nice flat you've got here!"

Adele's home may have been small, but it was very modern. Even she stopped to take an admiring look around when they came into the flat. The entrance opened straight into the living room, separated from the small corner kitchen by a low wall with counter space. Most of the apartment was painted white, with gray trim here and there. The walls, furniture, and other decor followed the same scheme, while the floor was paved with small lead-colored bricks. Two doors opened into the room: the bedroom and a large walk-in closet. When she'd bought the place, the closet had been a smaller, second bedroom. She'd had it converted. Between these two rooms, and connected to both, was the bathroom.

Adele had no intention of letting the man ogle the rest of her home. "On the couch," she said, and the two of them stretched Eric out on the sofa. More than asleep, her boss was now passed out. She lifted his legs to make sure he didn't fall to the floor, then put a pillow underneath his head.

The taxi driver snorted. "Bad thing that is, getting drunk like that. Happened to me once too. I can't even remember how I made it back home." Then he laughed, setting his broad belly jiggling.

Adele had no desire to entertain a conversation with the man. She took a twenty-pound note from her pocket. The other hand was inside her purse, fingering her gun. Better safe than sorry. "Here, please take this," she said, holding out the money.

The man looked at the bill, wavering. "No, no," he said, shaking his hands. "No need, miss."

"I insist," she said. "You were very kind to help." She accompanied these last words with the sincerest smile she could muster. Better to be very courteous to people who give you a helping hand. Her father had said as much a thousand times when she was growing up.

The Mentor

"Okay," said the man, taking the money reluctantly. "But . . ." He took a business card from the back pocket of his pants and handed it to Adele. "If you ever need to reserve a taxi, call me directly. That way you won't have to pay the company for the reservation."

Oh yes. There was always something to be gained from being courteous.

As soon as the taxi driver left, Adele turned all four locks on the door. She took off her jacket, hung it on a hook inside the closet, and picked up a blanket she kept folded on a shelf.

She went over to Eric, who was still sleeping peacefully on the couch, and covered him up with it. Even though it was late June, the nights could still be quite chilly. She didn't want him to catch cold. She took off his shoes, one after the other. Looking at him now, like this, he seemed truly fragile. Nothing like the powerful, self-assured man she saw walking around the department. The great Eric Shaw, a boss feared as much by his subordinates as by the criminals he hunted.

She laughed a little to herself at that thought, then went into the kitchen to boil some water. After that she went into her bedroom, got slowly undressed, and put on a pair of light pajamas, yawning as she went. She was more tired than she'd realized.

A little later, just as she was dropping her used bag of chamomile tea into the trash, her attention was drawn to some movement in the living room. She tiptoed over to the couch, abandoning her teacup on the table for the moment.

Eric had moved, uncovering himself a little, and now part of the blanket had slid down onto the floor.

Adele picked it up and spread it back over him. She ran her fingers through his hair, almost as if he were a child. His hair was thick and soft, a very light brown with just a faint dusting of white at the temples. She bent her head and gave his forehead the lightest of kisses.

Then she went and sat at the little table, taking back up her cup of tea while she watched her boss sleep on her couch.

He was a good-looking man. Apart from a little paunch and his tendency to neglect himself, he didn't seem at all like a fifty-year-old. She'd always had a thing for older men, but in reality she knew that he was too old for her. He could have been her father.

She took another sip, staring at him.

CHAPTER 4

He woke up with a terrible headache, accompanied by a firm willingness to kill himself in order to make it stop. The pleasant smell of coffee reached his nostrils, bringing him halfway back to reality. He felt disoriented. He couldn't figure out where he was; nothing around him seemed familiar. He could hear water running, but he couldn't tell if it was rain or faucet water.

A brief flash of people walking around Leicester Square leapt across his mind.

Where the hell was he?

He tried to pull himself upright, but the effort made him so dizzy that he gave up immediately.

"Good morning, boss."

Struggling, Eric recognized Adele's voice. Suddenly he realized he was still wearing the same clothes he'd had on last night, and that he was stretched out on a couch, half-covered with a blanket.

He tried to raise himself up again, this time more slowly.

The sound of running water stopped, and when Eric finally managed to sit upright, he could see that it came from a small corner kitchen at the end of the room. Standing in front of the sink, an enormous smile spread across her face, was Adele. She was wearing a white shirt and a pair of blue jeans. Sunlight flooded in through the window beside her and lit her up like a theater spotlight.

It was already daytime!

"Wh-what time is it?" stammered Eric. "Where am I?" he asked, even though he thought he already knew the answer. What he was really wondering was why he was there, how he had gotten there, and, most important of all, what had happened last night. He couldn't remember a thing. At least he'd woken up on a couch. That made him feel better.

"Don't worry, boss," said Adele, walking over to him and setting a mug of steaming coffee down on the table in front of the couch. "It's Sunday. You've got all the time you need to recover from your night on the town."

He wanted to say something witty in return, but he didn't know what to say and probably didn't have the strength to say it anyway.

In the meantime, Adele had disappeared again. He was so out of sorts that he didn't even see where she'd gone.

Eric reached out and took the mug. The smell of coffee was exhilarating, but there was no guarantee it would be enough to set him right again.

Adele reappeared at one of the two doors just as he was taking his first timid sips. She held up a packet of pills in one hand, then set it down on the little table in front of him without saying a word. Then she went back to the corner kitchen and filled a glass with water and brought that back as well. "Migraine, I assume," she said. Her tone of voice lay halfway between chastising and entertained.

He didn't need to answer. No doubt one good look at his face made it clear he had a hammering headache.

He swallowed a pill without even checking to see what it was. He wasn't sure he'd be able to read the fine print. He drank the entire glass of water, realizing his mouth was dry and racked by thirst. "Thanks," he muttered.

Adele was standing in front of the mirror, fixing her hair. "I'm sorry I brought you here. I tried to ask you where you live, but you weren't answering." She opened her purse and rummaged around in it.

"Goodness gracious," said Eric, rubbing his face with one hand. He was extremely embarrassed. "I hope I didn't do anything . . . anything that was . . ." Then he stopped, unsure how to proceed.

"Inopportune?" said Adele, laughing.

"Yeah. Something like that."

"Don't worry, boss. You were a perfect gentleman." She appeared to really be enjoying herself. She grabbed a linen jacket and put it on. "But now I've got to go. My sister-in-law is waiting for me so that she can give me the keys to her car." She headed for the door.

Eric was dumbfounded. He didn't know what she was expecting from him. Maybe he should get up and head home. Unfortunately, he was not at all sure he'd be able to stand.

He tried to open his mouth and say something, but she turned around and shushed him with a movement of her hand. "No, no . . . You take it easy. Make yourself at home." She pointed to one of the doors. "That's the bathroom. I left you a clean set of towels. The white ones, on the little cabinet." She took a key out of a drawer and set it by the telephone near the door. "When you leave, use this key to lock up," she said, pointing to one of the four locks on the door. "You can give it back to me when we see each other at the Yard, okay?"

After wading through that wave of instructions, which he'd tried to follow as closely as possible, it took him a few moments to realize that Adele was waiting for him to say something in return. "Oh . . . okay," was all he could muster. He must seem like a total idiot. "Thanks again," he managed at last.

"Don't worry about it, boss. See you soon." Then she winked at him, turned around, and left.

As soon as she was out of sight, Eric felt as if the enormous bubble he'd been sitting in burst open with no warning. The sounds of the morning flooding in through the partially open window overwhelmed him. He took another sip of coffee to clear his head and get a grip.

He had a hazy memory of the conversation they'd had while sitting on the little wall outside the pub. He'd asked her some very personal questions, perhaps too personal. He gave a little groan of disappointment with himself. Good God, how much had he had to drink? He remembered the first couple of beers. The third beer, which Adele had ordered, seemed to have opened a sort of chasm in his mind, one he'd tumbled into headfirst. It must have been spiked with something stronger. Maybe he should have asked what it was as soon as he'd realized it wasn't just beer, but something had stopped him. He didn't want to seem like an old man who was afraid of drinking something strong, or, even worse, someone who didn't know anything about the latest drink trends.

The point was he should have eaten something more. But it had been so exciting sitting there with her that he'd wound up spending more time talking than chewing.

Ridiculous, that's what it was. A man like him, in his position, losing his head over a young lady who, for all intents and purposes, was thoroughly entertained by the chance to torture him. Oh yes. That was convenient. Lay all the blame for his precocious midlife crisis on Adele. Pathetic. There were so many beautiful fortysomethings wandering around, and he had to go gaga over a twenty-seven-year-old. Sure, she was intelligent, and she seemed genuinely mature—she was just getting over a divorce too, after all. Most of all, she was extremely beautiful. But even all that couldn't justify his inability to maintain control.

He slapped his knees in an attempt to rise up out of his disappointment. Finally he managed to stand up.

He set the mug and the empty glass in the sink. It would be polite to wash and dry them, but he had no idea where things were in that kitchen and wasn't sure it would be a good idea to start digging around there anyway. Meanwhile, his swollen bladder woke up and started complaining, forcing him to head for the bathroom.

Unfamiliar with the flat, he opened the first door and found himself looking into the bedroom. The walls were peach colored, and the bed was covered with a similar, slightly darker-colored blanket. White curtains did little to block the sunlight flooding into the room, making it warm and welcoming. He immediately noticed the absence of any bureau or dresser. The room extended beyond the queen-sized bed, and he could see a desk with a portable computer on it. Its fan was blowing, telling him she'd left it turned on.

Curious, Eric went over to the computer. A video loop showing a storm-tossed sea ran across the screen over and over. The waves crashed on the beach, and surfers glided back and forth in the background, searching for the perfect wave.

Eric glanced around as if frightened at the prospect of being caught in the act of snooping on his colleague's computer; then he reached out to the mouse. The screen-saver video froze, and a little window popped up, requesting the password.

He wasn't really going to dig around in Adele's computer files, was he?

He was relieved he couldn't look any further. One less temptation.

Eric went back to looking around the room. There was something strange here, something he couldn't quite decipher, but he'd felt it back in the living room as well. A sense of the impersonal. Everything was beautiful, but on the whole it felt more like a hotel room than someone's personal living space. Maybe she'd only been here for a short time?

There was a photograph of Adele on almost every wall. They weren't traditional amateur photographs; they looked professional. There were close-ups, landscapes, and cityscapes. In one portrait of her, he could see the Eiffel Tower in the background.

Did she used to work as a model? That wouldn't surprise him.

Other than the photographs, there was nothing else that told him about the apartment's occupant. There were no images of her with other people—no friends, nothing of her ex-husband. No pictures of family or relatives. Everything seemed focused entirely, uniquely, on Adele. Beyond her, nothing. In a certain sense it fit with the image of herself she projected to others. Yet last night, for just a short while, Eric had begun to believe he was catching a glimpse of an entirely different woman. Now he was surprised to find he couldn't locate any trace of that woman here.

Oh, that's right. The bathroom. He'd gotten sidetracked, but his bladder brought him abruptly back to the here and now.

There was another door to the bedroom besides the one he'd come through. He opened it. Darkness. He tried flipping the switch alongside the doorway, and suddenly a dozen little halogen lights running around the ceiling lit the room up bright as day. The bathroom was embellished with tiles in all different shades of pastel green. It had a large bathtub and a shower, both very particular. They smacked of something *technological*. The entire room felt somehow projected into the future.

A large wall of mirrors facing him reproduced his own image, and he leaned in for a closer look. My God, he looked horrible. His face was shiny and pasty, dirtied with a five-o'clock shadow from the night before and sporting two deep, dark cavities where his eyes were supposed to be. His hair was mussed up. Who knew what absurd positions he'd tossed and turned into while asleep.

Eric went to the toilet. He required a few extra moments to focus on his next move, but finally the valves opened and he managed to empty his bladder, and with it the world seemed like a better place.

A large white towel lay on the cabinet, carefully folded. He picked it up and looked around the shower. It was large enough to fit two people comfortably and looked inviting enough. She'd told him to make himself at home, hadn't she?

* * *

The pungent odor of chemicals mixed with decomposing flesh invaded Eric's nose and mouth the moment he walked into the morgue, making him cough.

"Good morning, Detective," said Dr. Dawson, who was busy filling out a file. He said this without so much as glancing up from his paperwork. The body of Nicholas Thompson was stretched out on the autopsy table. His clothes had been removed, but the examination hadn't started yet. Two red plastic batons were sticking out of the body. One was sticking up perpendicular from his groin; the other ran out from the side of his neck.

"Richard," said Shaw, returning the doctor's salutations.

A flash illuminated the body for a split second, revealing the presence of a third person in the room with them. Eric stiffened a little, recognizing Adele. She, on the other hand, appeared to be entirely focused on her work and uninterested in his arrival.

"Good morning," murmured Eric. Adele nodded to him and flashed a small smile. She always behaved this way; it was nothing new, save for the fact that the previous morning he'd woken up in her apartment, on her couch, instead of in his own home, and that made him embarrassed. "What can you tell me about the victim?" he asked, turning back to the doctor, thinking it best to focus on the case.

"First of all, as you can see, the guesswork conducted at the crime scene was mostly inaccurate."

"What do you mean?" Eric went to the table to look at the body up close.

"We thought the assassin shot the victim in the neck first, then in the groin in order to leave him to die from blood loss." The doctor set his file down on a little cart, then finally turned to look the head of the scientific investigations department squarely in the eye. "But the direction of the two bullets tells us a different story." He pointed to the baton in the victim's neck. "As you can see, this baton is pointing downward with respect to the rest of the body."

"That means the assassin was shorter than the victim and had to raise his arm to shoot. Although . . ." Eric paused for a moment, noting the size of the cadaver. "The victim can't be more than a little over five tall, if that."

"The bullet wound is less than sixty degrees. That tells us the shot was taken from below. Things get more complicated when we look at the groin."

Eric's attention moved to the red baton sticking straight up out of Thompson's groin. "It's at a ninety-degree angle!"

"Exactly. Either our assassin is a dwarf, or a child. Or he was sitting much lower when he shot the victim." The doctor had the air of someone who loved to puzzle over riddles.

Another flash from the camera lit up the room.

"Maybe there was a fight," Shaw said. "The assassin fell on . . . the couch, and shot from there." It was an acceptable theory.

Thompson wasn't very tall, but he was relatively beefy. He would have had the strength to push away another person, even someone bigger than he was.

While they thought about this, Eric noticed from the corner of his eye that Adele had set down the camera and picked up a tablet computer. She was moving her left index finger around the screen.

"I don't know what your team will find on the scene or in the victim's clothing," said Dawson. "But I can tell you this: there are no signs of injuries or struggle on the body. It doesn't look like he fought with anyone before he died."

"Then how do you think it went down?" Eric asked.

"Hell if I know!" exclaimed the doctor, lifting up both arms. "I'm just your simple, everyday pathologist." That made Eric smile. He'd heard Dawson say the same thing at least a hundred times. "You criminologists are the wizards of reconstruction. But before we get to that, there's one other thing I didn't tell you." He stooped down to pick up something from one of the lower trays on the cart. A moment later he was holding a clear plastic bag in front of Eric's face, smiling with satisfaction.

Eric tried to focus on the tiny piece of colored plastic that sat inside the bag.

"I'll save you the trouble of asking," said Dawson, before Eric could even formulate a question. "It's a piece of adhesive tape. I found it here." He pushed the victim's head to one side and pointed a gloved finger at a spot toward the back of the cheek. "What with all the blood, we didn't notice it the first time around. It only appeared once I cleaned the body."

"He'd been gagged with tape!" This changed things.

"Exactly." It was clearly Dawson's favorite word. "So it's no longer clear that he was shot in the neck to silence his yell before being shot in the groin. In fact, just the opposite may be true." The doctor removed his glasses and lifted the head, turning it back so that the eyes looked upward. "Our talented Miss Pennington has an interesting theory about the way the homicide unfolded; it fits perfectly with what we can see on the body."

Eric and Dawson both looked at Adele, who seemed to have been waiting for the two men to get around to talking to her.

"I've created a simulation," she said, holding up the tablet she was using, but with the screen facing away from them. She sounded very sure of herself.

Eric hesitated for a moment, unsure whether or not to approach her. This is why it wasn't a good idea to fraternize with colleagues. He felt embarrassed for gestures that under any other circumstances would have felt perfectly normal. Except that there hadn't been any real fraternization between them. Nothing had happened. It was all in his head. He kept telling himself that and glanced at the doctor.

"She's all yours," said the doctor. What a strange choice of words. Eric almost gasped. "I've already seen it," continued the doctor; then he put his glasses back on and went back to his file.

A little reluctantly, Shaw walked around the table and stood next to Adele. She moved her head a little, then waved one hand in front of her face as if to chase away a bug. He couldn't see any bugs there, but the gesture sent a wave of her perfume wafting his way, overpowering the stench of dead flesh, if only for a moment.

"This is a reconstruction of the crime scene. It's pretty rudimentary," said Adele, almost apologizing beforehand.

The image on the screen was a three-dimensional reconstruction of the room in which they'd found the body. Roughly three feet away from the table, down on the floor, were two large bloodstains, one of which was roughly three times larger than the other. They weren't round, but irregular, as if someone had prevented the blood from spreading out evenly. It was a very realistic reconstruction. Eric recognized the scene. All that was missing was the body.

"At first we thought that the victim was here, more or less, when he was shot," Adele continued. A human figure materialized alongside the larger bloodstain.

"No, wait," Eric interrupted. "If that were the case, we'd have high-velocity splatter marks all around the body, and gravitational drops where the body fell."

"That's right, and in fact there weren't any," she responded. "When we lifted the body up, most of the flooring underneath it was clean. That made me think Thompson wasn't standing at all when he was shot."

"Hold on." Eric knew where Adele was going with this. "You think he was already on the floor."

"That would explain the shape of the bloodstain, and the fact that the stain near the neck was moved with respect to the body," said Adele, nodding.

Now Eric was a little lost. They'd thought the unusual position of the bloodstain was due to the fact that the victim had wriggled as he was dying.

"I'll show you." Adele fingered an icon on the side of the screen, and the position of the body changed. Now the human figure was no longer standing but lying down on the floor. "If they shot him when he was already lying on the floor, that would explain the direction of the bullets first and foremost."

A new figure, this one armed with a gun, stood alongside the victim, its feet by the victim's groin.

"The assassin threatens him with a gun, forces him to gag himself . . ." Adele's account was fluid. It was clear she'd been working on it for a while. Given that it was nine o'clock on Monday morning, she must have been working on it during the weekend. "Then he makes the victim lie down on the floor, and *bang!*"—she raised her voice to imitate the shot—"he shoots him in the groin."

Without meaning to, Eric winced, instinctively moving his hands to cover his private parts. He caught ahold of himself in time, stopping his hands halfway there. The movement didn't escape Adele, who shot him a malicious glance. He wondered for a moment if she'd done it on purpose to see his reaction.

"Thompson wants to scream," Adele continued. "But since he's gagged, he can't produce anything more than soft noises, something the neighbors can't hear."

"But nobody heard the shots either," said Eric. He was still her boss and had every right to test her a little when the opportunity arrived.

"He used a silencer," said Adele.

Okay. That was easy enough. They'd decided as much back when they were examining the crime scene.

"So . . . he shot him in the groin." Eric tried to mimic the shot, holding his arm down and pointing at the floor. "The victim instinctively brought his hands to his groin, and in doing so curled up a little on one side."

Adele smiled, satisfied, and touched the tablet again, moving on to the next sequence. The body was now in a fetal position, curled up on one side. The assassin's arm pointed downward, aiming at the victim's neck. "Bang." A single line united the pistol and the penetration wound on one side of the neck.

The detective again examined the corpse stretched out on the table. The angle corresponded to the angle of the baton. But there was still something missing. "But that's not how the body was when we found it."

Adele had an answer ready. "Because it was moved."

"How can you tell?"

"The assassin waited until his victim was dead," she said, apparently ignoring Eric's question. "He struck the carotid artery in full, so he didn't have to wait long. Thompson ran out of blood quickly and must have lost consciousness almost immediately." She shifted her attention from the tablet to the corpse. "He pushed the body with one foot, shifting Thompson again onto his back." The same sequence played out virtually on the screen, and Adele pointed to the side of the body where there was a bluish stain beneath the skin. "It wasn't visible at first, but after a day in the fridge, this perimortem bruise showed up."

"He did it with his shoe." They were dealing with the kind of revelations that—when all the clues began to line up one after the other, making it possible to see the threads connecting the whole—made Eric remember why he loved his job so deeply. He put on a pair of latex gloves and touched the flesh around the bruise. "It seems a lot more marked toward the center."

"As if it were the result of a kick made with a rigid, pointed shoe," Adele suggested. They had both reached the same conclusion. "Like a woman's shoe."

"Ah, a woman!" exclaimed the doctor from the other side of the room.

"And once the body was stretched out on the floor," said Eric, "the killer ripped off the tape."

"At that point there was no longer risk of him screaming," Adele concluded, triumph in her eyes.

Five minutes later they were standing in the atrium, waiting for the elevator. Adele was fingering her tablet again. Eric was watching her. At a certain point it seemed as if she was about to look up at him, and Eric quickly focused on his wristwatch. Exactly thirty seconds had passed since the last time he'd checked it.

He snorted at his own stupidity, nearly certain he saw Adele stifle a laugh. He couldn't be sure of it, but he also didn't dare look in her direction.

Suddenly he remembered the key. He patted his pants pockets, finally pulling out the long key. He held it out to her, ready to thank her again, when she abruptly interrupted him.

"Did you enjoy snooping around my house, boss?"

Eric was stunned. "What?" For a split second he was afraid Adele had a video surveillance system. His hand, holding the key, was frozen halfway between them. It took him a beat to remember that he hadn't done anything wrong. Except maybe touching the mouse. Adele's snarky expression erased any lingering doubts.

She was kidding.

Adele took the key, her fingers brushing his hand. At that very moment the doors to the elevator opened. Miriam and Jane were standing inside.

Eric and Adele were caught both holding the key between them. Miriam's expression hardened, while Jane's mouth split into a smile. Shaw quickly dropped the key and got busy adjusting his wrist lapels.

"Just the man we were looking for," exclaimed Jane, stepping out of the elevator. She squinted in an expression of disdain.

In the meantime, Adele had gone back to fiddling with her tablet and stepped quickly into the elevator. Miriam glared at her crosswise, then exited after Jane. Adele reached out, pressed a button, and the door closed.

Miriam Leroux was staring at Eric insistently. "They told us you were in the morgue. Discover anything interesting?"

Despite the question, he had the distinct impression the young detective wasn't all that interested in the investigation just then.

"Did you see Adele's reconstruction?" asked Jane. "Amazing, isn't it?"

Miriam skewered her with a glare, but Jane ignored her companion.

"Yes, well . . ." Eric paused for a moment. When he'd arrived at the office, he hadn't seen Jane, and then he'd gone straight down to the morgue. How did she know about the reconstruction?

Then his second in command raised her hand with her smartphone in it. "She sent it to me five minutes ago."

"Sooner or later I'm going to have to buy one of those infernal things too," he admitted. Yes. Talking was a good idea. "Lately I've had the impression that I'm always one step behind the rest of you."

Jane laughed, and even Miriam seemed to relax a little. But she still didn't seem like she was in much of a good mood.

"Don't be silly, Eric," said the criminologist, slapping him on the back. "You're always two steps ahead of the rest of us put together. Don't you think?" she concluded, turning to Miriam.

"So, what's the news?" said Leroux.

"Appears we're looking for a woman," said Eric, giving her an authoritative stare. It seemed like just the other day he was giving Miriam dolls for her birthday. He had been a sort of uncle to her, practically a member of the family, but that didn't give her the right to behave like this in the workplace.

"A woman?" Miriam's curiosity seemed to get the better of her outrage.

"It looks like he was kicked with a woman's shoe," explained Eric. "Of course it could be a man wearing pointy shoes, but this element along with the shot to the groin gives us something to think about."

"An abused victim? Rape?" The detective's hand moved to the hilt of her pistol. She moved her head a little in a sort of nervous tic, then let go of the gun and straightened out her arm again.

"You tell me," he responded.

"We haven't found anything like that in Johnson's past yet," said Miriam, massaging her right wrist. "But maybe we should dig a little deeper."

"An extremely meticulous woman who loves tea," said Jane. She had listened to them in silence up until that point. The other two turned to look at her. The criminologist showed them a photograph on her cell phone. They could see a table with an empty teacup on it. Jane swiped to the next photo: two tea filters in the garbage. "Evidently two people drank tea that day." She paused briefly for effect. "But we only found one teacup."

"Maybe Thompson just loved really strong tea," said Eric, shouldering the role of devil's advocate.

Jane lifted up a finger to silence him. "We checked the dish rack and found four other teacups and four little plates just like this one. Add the one on the table, and you've got five. Looks like the set's missing a pair."

Now he understood what she was driving at. "The killer took everything he or she used so as not to leave any evidence behind."

"Or DNA," concluded his second in command.

"No fool, this one," Miriam added.

Eric crossed his arms over his chest. "No," he said. "Not one bit."

CHAPTER 5

She pulled the yellow ribbon off the doorway and walked inside, leaving the door open behind her. The crime scene had already been picked over and sifted through down to the last square inch. The scientific investigations department had sequestered and catalogued everything that might have proven useful, photographing the minutest details in the room. Soon they would let the landlord back in to clean up, and then there wouldn't be any signs left of what had happened here.

Miriam paused to look at the bloodstains on the floor. It was no surprise no one in the building had heard anything. People were undoubtedly busy with their everyday lives and wouldn't have been able to distinguish a muffled cry or the sound of a silenced shot from a thousand other sounds coming from nearby apartments, televisions, or traffic in the streets outside.

But maybe someone had seen some detail, one that appeared unimportant but that might acquire new meaning when analyzed in the right context.

A noise in the hallway outside made her spin around. She couldn't see where it had come from, but it was followed by excited clatter.

"Sayyid, quit it with that ball!" shouted a woman's voice, echoing down the corridor. "And stop running on the stairs!"

Detective Leroux stuck her head out of the victim's apartment and nearly took a soccer ball to the face as it whipped past her. The ball bounced down the hall and a boy, roughly ten years old, shot past her like a streak of lightning, chasing the ball.

"Hey, kid!" said Miriam instinctively, trying in vain to stop him. "Be careful!"

She followed the boy. He'd come to a stop in front of a door. He was holding the ball in both hands, staring back at her, frightened.

"Who are you? Leave my son alone."

Miriam turned around and faced the woman speaking. She was roughly forty years old, just now coming up the steps. She was wearing a long dress and a dark shirt that was tightly buttoned up her torso. She wore a veil on her head that hung down and covered her neck as well. She was carrying two large grocery bags, one in each hand. They seemed quite heavy, and the woman struggled to reach the top of the stairs. When she made it onto their floor, she had to stop and lean on the banister to catch her breath.

"Good afternoon, ma'am," said Miriam in a cordial tone, walking toward her. She took her badge out of her pocket and held it out to the woman. "Detective Miriam Leroux, Metropolitan Police."

This last phrase brought a grimace to the other woman's face. "You again," she said as she started walking again. "We didn't see anything. We didn't hear anything. I already told all of this to your colleague." She reached Miriam and, without looking at the detective, pushed past her and headed for her son.

"I'm sorry. I hope you don't mind, but if I could just ask, Miss . . . ?"

The woman sighed noisily, set the bags down on the floor, and started searching for something in the purse slung over one shoulder. "Jassim," she said.

Sayyid said nothing. As soon as his mother reached his side, he hid behind her and peeked out from time to time to see what the detective was doing. Now he was holding the ball under one arm, while the other hand gripped his mother's side.

"Miss Jassim, would you mind if I asked your son a few questions?"

The woman, who had fished out her house keys in the meantime and stuck them into the lock, turned around and shot the detective a look of annoyance. "Why?"

"As I'm sure you know, a man was murdered in the apartment next to yours. Maybe Sayyid saw someone go in or come out. Does he often play out here in the hallway?"

Miss Jassim turned to her son and shot him a look of reproof. It almost seemed as if she were blaming him for the fact that she was now stuck talking to the detective in front of her.

Going over to them, Miriam bent down so that her eyes were at the same level as Sayyid's. "Do you often play out here in the hallway, Sayyid?"

The boy said nothing.

"Answer the lady!" his mother implored.

Sayyid looked first at his mother, then back at Miriam. Then he nodded, clutching his mother's wrist with his hands.

Detective Leroux smiled at him. "That's fine. Did you see anyone new enter or leave your neighbor's apartment?"

The child stared at her. He was almost trembling.

"There's nothing to be afraid of. You can talk to me. I'm with the police."

This didn't appear to calm the boy one bit. "I-I don't know . . ." he stammered.

"You don't know? Try to think about it a little. I don't know . . . maybe a lady, for example?"

Sayyid squinted for a moment. "Yes," he said, practically whispering.

"Goodness gracious!" exclaimed the mother. "Behave yourself. Tell the lady what you saw. And pull yourself together!" She forced Sayyid to let go of her and stand on his own.

"I saw a woman come out of there," he said, pointing to Thompson's apartment.

"When?"

"I don't remember."

"Okay. Had you ever seen her before?"

Sayyid shook his head no.

"What do you remember about her? Was she short, tall . . . ?"

"Tall!"

"As tall as me?" asked Miriam, standing up straight and pointing to herself. "Or taller? Or not as tall?"

The boy hesitated for a moment, then looked away from the policewoman. "Like you . . ."

"Okay, Sayyid." She bent down to his level again, bringing her face just inches from his, forcing him to look right at her. "Do you remember what she looked like?"

The boy swallowed nervously. "She was dressed in black. And she wore a big pair of sunglasses."

"What color was her hair?"

The boy shrugged.

"Would you recognize her, if you saw her again?"

Sayyid immediately shook his head forcefully.

"Okay," said Miriam, sighing.

"Do you need us much longer?" asked the mother, sounding bored. "My son has to do his homework."

The detective stood up again. "Of course," she said. "You're right." She smiled to the woman and took a step back.

Miss Jassim turned the key in the lock and opened the door.

"Just one last thing," Detective Leroux added.

Miriam's voice interrupted the other woman's movement. The child had set the ball down on the floor and put both hands on the door in order to push his way in, but his mother had a firm grip on the knob and kept Sayyid from slipping inside.

"When the woman came out of the apartment, what did she do after that?"

Sayyid stopped pushing on the door and looked at her, but he didn't answer.

"Did she leave right away, or did she do something else before she left?" insisted the detective.

"She locked the door behind her," the boy said.

Then the mother let go of the doorknob and Sayyid ran inside.

The cell phone rang right as the light turned green. Miriam pressed the answer button on the steering wheel and accelerated hard, cutting off the car to her left in the process, tires screeching. A car horn honked behind her.

"Leroux," she answered.

"Detective, this is Mills. I investigated that thing you were asking about, and I may have found something interesting," said a male voice coming through her speakers.

Just as she was overtaking a bus, a pedestrian stepped out into the street ahead of her, forcing Miriam to screech to a stop. *Merde!* she swore in French.

"Everything okay?" asked her colleague, preoccupied.

Miriam took off again. "Yes, everything's okay. You were saying?"

"After digging around in Thompson's past, I found an old accusation for rape."

She was now out on a four-lane road and became more relaxed behind the wheel. "Oh yeah? How come it's only surfacing now?"

"Because it dates back to when he was still a minor, and the charges were dropped, so they don't show up in the system. I asked a friend over in the juvenile sector to check him out, just to be sure, and then this thing popped up."

"Tell me more about it," she said as a drop of sweat threaded its way down from her temple. Miriam wiped it away with one hand and turned up the air-conditioning. The sun was right in her face, bothering her.

"A schoolmate he'd gone on a date with during his last year of high school came back home in tears and confessed to her parents that Thompson had forced her to have sex with him."

Miriam patted her pockets, searching for a pair of sunglasses, before realizing that they were perched on her head. She put them on. Much better.

"But it was his word against the girl's, and she didn't exactly have the reputation of a saint, if you catch my meaning." There was a deep breath on the other end of the phone. "Besides, we're talking about more than forty years ago . . ."

"So the girl decided to drop it," murmured Detective Leroux. Her head twitched a little with her tic.

"Yeah, but that doesn't mean it wasn't true."

Nauseated, Miriam closed her eyes for a moment. When she opened them again she was facing the red brake lights of the car in front of her. She slammed on her brakes, barely stopping in time.

The voice on the other end of the phone continued. "And if he was raping women back then, maybe he's done it other times. It's hard to know exactly what he's done. All we know is that he's never been identified and caught before."

"That's possible. What about the girl? Can you track her down?" Miriam's stomach churned. She opened the glove compartment and took out a little foil-wrapped package of pills and stuck one in her mouth, dropping the packet in her lap.

"I did," said Mills in a discouraged tone. "She died six months ago. Cancer."

"Fuck . . ." Miriam shifted into first and took off again.

"Yeah."

"Did she have a daughter, by any chance?"

"Hmm . . . I don't have anything on that, but if you want I'll double-check."

"Good. Do that. We'll catch up later." Miriam ended the conversation and turned onto a side street.

CHAPTER 6

The video ran quickly across the screen, colors from the images brightening the room. The sun had already gone down, and the last faint rays of daylight barely illuminated the window frame.

Eric flipped the light switch. When the fluorescent overheads flickered on, Stern jumped in his seat.

"Jesus, boss! You scared the shit out of me!"

"Sleep much, Martin?" asked Shaw, a hint of disapproval in his voice.

"No, no. Of course not!" Stern leapt to his feet, practically standing to salute. "I was watching some surveillance video we picked up from a camera near the building where Thompson's apartment is. There's footage from a jewelry store right next to the building's entrance." He pointed to a screen in front of him.

"The other stuff is from an ATM machine across the street." He adjusted his shriveled T-shirt. It was as if he'd thrown it on as soon as it came out of the dryer. There was an enormous silhouette of Darth Vader on the chest. He nodded at the other screen, which was darker and displayed close-ups of a man withdrawing cash. "The building door is right in line with the video camera, but it's always out of focus. Unfortunately, that's all we've got."

"Have you found anything?" Eric put one hand on Stern's shoulder and squeezed, pushing him gently into his chair and back to work. He enjoyed putting the screws on Stern. Even though he had been with the department for four years, he continued to kowtow to Eric, which only brought more ribbing from Detective Shaw. Shaw hoped that, with enough prodding, eventually the man would start standing up for himself. Stern was good at what he did, but he lacked courage and character.

Martin's face contracted, then he whistled softly. "Well . . . I've been watching this footage of the days when we think the crime may have been committed. I'm into the third day now, and so far no woman dressed in black has come out of or gone into the building. At least not during the daytime."

"The witness says he saw her while he was playing in the hallway. The sun sets late these days. I doubt he was playing at night."

"Oh. Yeah. I'll keep looking. If this woman really exists, she had to have passed through that doorway." His mouth sprung open in a wide yawn.

"You're never going to find her with your eyes closed!" said Eric sarcastically. "That's enough for today. It's late. You can start back up again tomorrow." Then he left the room.

"Your wish is my command, boss," said Stern, but his voice was already fading as Eric moved into the main laboratory.

The room was empty. As usual, he'd stayed in the office longer than he should have. Everyone else had already gone home, except for Martin.

"Good night!" Martin called out.

Stern's outline went racing down the corridor. He'd undoubtedly stayed late to show that he was taking the job seriously, and now that he'd gotten the green light to head home, he wasn't going to waste a minute.

The sound of something rolling turned Eric around, just in time to see a pen fall off the edge of a desk.

He sighed. He was truly the only one left. A little earlier he'd caught a glimpse of Adele walking past his door, and he'd struggled to resist the desire to follow her and talk to her. What would he have said to her anyway?

He'd thought about that for a good hour; then he simply stood up from his desk and left his office, but there was no sign of her anywhere.

Ultimately that was for the best. If he tried to approach her, even simply as a friend, he risked making himself look even more ridiculous than he already had.

He walked across the laboratory to the little staff room where people had coffees and snacks on their breaks. The light was on, but the room was empty. Then he headed for the ballistics lab, but well before he got there he could see it was closed with no signs of life.

Eric looked at his watch. It was almost ten thirty. He'd eaten a sandwich a couple of hours earlier, thinking he'd stay in the office awhile and take care of a few things. Now it was probably time to head home.

He walked back to his office to grab his jacket. Just as he passed a door to the locker room, he heard another noise.

Eric stopped and listened carefully. It was something metallic, maybe the handle of a locker, but the light inside the room was turned off. He stuck his head in. Light from the corridor slipped in, making the room almost entirely visible save a few shadowy corners.

He walked in, making his way past the benches. Everything seemed okay.

He reached the end of a row of lockers and was about to turn around when he noticed a dark outline out of the corner of his eye— Eric caught just a glimpse of the shadow before it crashed into him.

He found himself holding Adele in his arms.

"Gee whiz, boss!" He could feel her grow tense, her body stiffening. "What the hell are you doing in here?"

He had his hands on her arms, unsure what to say next. "I . . . I heard a noise. I didn't think anyone was still here. The light's turned off."

Exactly, goddamn it. What on earth was she doing in the locker room in the dark?

"I forgot my tablet," said Adele. She pulled away from him and took a step back. "I came back to pick it up. I'm used to moving around in the dark."

"Sorry if I scared you," Eric said, getting a grip on himself. "I thought I was the only one still here."

Adele's alarmed expression melted away, leaving a half-smile in its wake. Or at least that's how it seemed to him from what little he could see in the dim light. "No big deal," she said.

Eric moved to let her pass, and Adele headed to the door.

"You should go home, boss." She waved to him as she walked out.

He nibbled on his upper lip. What had she been doing in here? He summoned his courage and jogged after her. "I wanted to apologize for the other night," he said when he caught up with her.

Adele looked perplexed. "For what?" She didn't seem to know what he was talking about.

"You know what I mean," he said, challenging her with his eyes.

She sighed. A light of understanding flickered in her eyes. "If you're afraid I might tell somebody about your *misadventure* . . ." She smiled. "Don't worry." Then she made as if to turn around again.

"That's not what I meant," he said, stepping to block her path.

That seemed to try her patience. "Listen, boss. You don't have anything to apologize for, really. Everything's fine." Adele said it as if she gathered up people so drunk they passed out cold in taxicabs and brought them home with her every night—as if it was nothing at all to her. But that approach only increased Eric's discomfort. He felt a growing sense of anger every time she told him how little it mattered.

"Okay," he said at length. "If you say so."

She slapped her boss on the shoulder. "Good night, boss," she said, then turned to go.

"I guess you must have paid the tab then. Or am I remembering that wrong? I certainly don't remember paying." He couldn't recall much from that evening, to tell the truth.

"Oh, don't worry about it." She kept walking. "You didn't have to. It's my pub," she added, raising her voice as she stepped into the elevator.

Her pub? Oh, of course. Her ex worked there. Maybe they owned the place. He couldn't help but feel disappointed. It would have been better if he had never talked to her in the first place. Adele Pennington had a gift for making others feel diminished somehow. He'd watched her exert this effect over his colleagues, and now he felt it himself. All this should have annoyed him, but deep inside he knew it only made her more interesting to him, precisely because she was so hard to get a handle on.

Of course she was much younger than he was, but she was hardly a little girl.

After finally slipping out of the station, Eric made his way toward the St. James's Park station. Just as he was stepping into the tube station entrance, he noticed a red car pull up along the side of the road. The window rolled down. Before he could see who was driving, he heard a voice he recognized.

"Do you want a lift, boss?"

"I imagine you're enjoying yourself." Eric squinted at her as the car came to a stop.

"Where can I take you?" asked Adele, ignoring his comment.

"Marylebone, York Street," he said as he climbed into the car. "I'll tell you where to stop."

She turned left onto Victoria Street. "You're in my neighborhood."

"I know."

Adele displayed an ambiguous smile but didn't say anything.

"Oh yes, you're clearly enjoying this," said Eric.

"I'm sorry?"

"You know what I'm talking about." He adjusted his seat belt so that he could turn and look straight at her. "I've been watching you during the past few months in the office."

"Oh yeah?" There was a shade of impertinence in Adele's voice, and that only irritated him further.

"You do everything you can to make your colleagues' lives difficult. You draw attention to their faults, cut them down in public. You're so good at it that the more insecure ones start to believe it's their fault." While he talked, he studied her face for any reaction, but Adele was impassive, almost disinterested—except for her eyelids, which twitched nervously. She was listening to him, he was certain of this. "And now you're trying to do the same with me."

Adele said nothing, but she accelerated suddenly in order to over-take a bus that had pulled over to off-load passengers. "I don't know what you're talking about."

Eric snorted sarcastically. "I don't know why you do it. You're good at what you do. You don't have to prove anything. Yet you keep putting up walls between yourself and your colleagues. The more time passes, the higher those barriers become, and I'm trying to understand why."

"Listen!" she exclaimed, finally displaying some annoyance. "I don't have to be friends with everyone, and regardless, the way I interact with the people around me is none of your business. You're not my father, and I'm not a suspect in some case you're investigating. You have no right to give me the third degree."

"But I *am* your boss, and the way you behave on the job is my business."

"Right now we're in *my* car, not in your department."

"So you'd rather we had this conversation back at the Yard, in front of the entire team?"

She bit back a response and took a long, deep breath.

Eric smiled to himself. He didn't exactly enjoy using his position to lord over his colleagues, but this time he was glad it was an option.

"Who knows what the others would think if they knew how hard it is for you to handle a few beers," she responded with a biting tone.

"Ha!" said Eric, who was expecting exactly this sort of attack. "After your little joke this week, I think that most people are convinced we're sleeping together, so I doubt that little tidbit would shock them all that much."

Adele laughed.

Oh yes, she was clearly enjoying this. "To tell you the truth," he continued, "I should thank you. It seems to have earned me nothing but admiration."

"You wish," murmured Adele.

Eric shook his head. He'd opened a door between them, but now the conversation had taken a turn he didn't like at all. The problem was that Adele was right. She'd understood quite clearly what he was thinking about, but she wouldn't give him the satisfaction. Right now he was so angry that he'd lost all interest in her as a woman. She was one heck of a bitch all right. In his own mind he'd unconsciously defended her when he'd heard the things other people were saying about her, but now he was facing his own arrogance.

The worst thing was that, despite this, he still felt attracted to her, even now. His anger only heightened his desire.

The car turned onto York Street, and Adele turned one eloquent, arched eyebrow his way.

"Pull over at the second intersection," said Eric. His time was almost up, and he wanted to end the conversation in a civil manner. "You're an excellent criminologist, I have to admit that, but our job doesn't end in the laboratory. Your relationship with your colleagues is important too, especially if you want to further your career."

"I'd rather concentrate on the science in order to further my career, instead of grasping for *help* somewhere else."

Eric felt that was a low blow. His relatively unorthodox methods weren't exactly a secret, but they were tolerated, sometimes even encouraged, as long as no one else was involved. Everybody knew full well that his aim wasn't to advance his career or burnish his reputation with the higher-ups in the Metropolitan Police Service for favors down the road. His only mission was to guarantee that guilty parties were brought to justice, no matter the cost. It had become his life mission, and to have her throw it back at him was irksome and cheap.

The car stopped. "Good night, boss," said Adele, her voice dry and matter of fact.

Detective Shaw looked at her, uncertain. Did she really want to end the conversation here? She looked straight ahead. Finally Eric unlatched his seat belt and opened the door.

"You're right," she said, her voice so soft that he could barely hear it as he rose out of the car. He turned to meet her stare.

"You don't know anything about my life," she continued. "This is a really stressful time for me, and *maybe* I've been taking my problems out on the wrong people."

He had nothing to say in return. It was true: when all was said and done, he really didn't know a thing about her. Every opinion he had, whether good or bad, was influenced by feelings he wasn't supposed to be entertaining. For the first time ever, it occurred to him that things would be better if they didn't work together at all.

"But you're wrong about one thing." The dome light glowed a dim yellow on Adele's face. It almost looked like there were tears in her eyes. "I don't enjoy it at all." But the half-smile that accompanied the statement seemed to say just the opposite.

Adele leaned over the passenger seat and closed the door, practically jerking it out of his hands. Then she left.

Eric stood there for a moment on the sidewalk, watching Adele drive away. His jaw was clenched, and his hands curled into fists. He couldn't be sure, but he thought he could feel Adele's eyes on him in the rearview mirror. He could certainly imagine them.

It was quicker than he was. He tried to run even faster, but his legs were barely responding anymore. He gasped for breath, hardly getting air into his lungs. He hadn't been much of a runner even when he was younger, and what little ability he had had only diminished with age. Every once in a while he looked over his shoulder. The shadow was still following him; it wasn't all in his head. It didn't even need to run. It was faster than he was.

He turned into an alley. He didn't know this part of the city that well, but maybe he could find a place to hide.

There was a soft, muted sound behind him. Tiny shards of cement flew off the wall beside him. A gunshot without a bang. He put a foot in a pothole and found himself sprawled out on the pavement. He could feel his heart racing in his chest. He couldn't get back up again. He didn't have the strength to run anymore.

Footsteps behind him. Then his pursuer stopped.

He put his hands on his head, as if that might save him, but he couldn't resist the temptation to look. His pursuer was still partly concealed in shadow. He couldn't see the face, but now he understood why he hadn't heard the shot: a long silencer was fastened onto the barrel of the pistol.

"Get up!"

"Please, I'm begging you. Don't hurt me. You can have all my money."

Another bullet. This one struck the ground to his right, grazing him.

"No, fuck! Okay, okay!" He was whimpering. He'd wet himself, but he didn't care about that now. He just wanted to get out, to save himself. He began praying as he struggled to get to his feet. If he didn't die tonight, he swore he would behave for the rest of his life. But then, how many times had he made that promise before? Promises made and broken.

His pursuer took a step forward into the light pouring down from a street lamp overhead. He could see the person's face.

He didn't understand. Who the hell was this?

"Turn around."

Whoever it was, there was a working gun in one hand, and so he did as he was told. But he couldn't help from asking: "Who are you . . . ?"

"Death."

He didn't even have enough time to hear the response. His back was consumed with fire. A viscous liquid filled his mouth. Then everything disappeared.

CHAPTER 7

After having spent the previous day and the whole morning watching videos without knowing precisely what he was looking for, Stern was sick and tired of that damn entrance to the apartment building and the carousel of humanity that came in and out of it. There was no sign whatsoever of the mysterious madam dressed in black. Maybe she put a jacket on over her clothing and he'd missed her, or maybe the witness wasn't remembering her correctly. After all, he was just a kid.

He could feel his eyes burning. Why was he always stuck with the crappy tasks? He wished he could just once go out into the field, but they kept telling him he wasn't ready, that he was at his best in front of a computer. It was true that nobody else on the team was as good as he was in that area, but sooner or later he wanted to become important. When he'd started working in scientific investigations, he'd imagined he'd be given much more exciting assignments. But more often than not, he wound up here, taking people off the list of suspects—or worse yet, not finding a single thing. Just like now.

Then it happened.

Stern leaned forward to see more clearly, knocking a file off the table. He ignored it. Using his mouse, he rewound the video and stopped it. Then he brought up another window, going roughly half an hour back in time.

It was clearly the same person, but there was something strange.

Eric's cell phone rang just as he was walking back into the office after his lunch break, though it was hard to consider a sandwich eaten standing up and a quick coffee at Starbucks an actual lunch. He held his coffee cup in one hand and fished around in his jacket pocket for the phone with the other. It was a delicate balancing act, but finally he managed to pull it out.

"Shaw," he said, biting back a curse when a few scalding drops splashed out over the rim and burned his hand.

"Agent Gavin Lennox here. City Police."

Eric put what was left of his coffee down on the desk and, holding the cell phone against one shoulder, wiped his hand clean with a Kleenex. "What can I do for you, Agent Lennox?"

The City of London neighborhood was the only section of the metropolis that didn't fall under Scotland Yard's jurisdiction. It had a relatively small population and was filled mostly with office buildings, including some of the city's tallest, like London's famous Gherkin building. The City Police often collaborated with the Metropolitan Police, but it was rare for the scientific investigations department to be contacted directly.

"I've got a murder case that might be connected with one of yours," Lennox said.

"Why are you calling me?" Eric flopped down in his chair, his curiosity piqued. "You should get in touch with the detective handling it in homicide."

"I'm calling you because this is directly related to scientific investigations. We've got a ballistics report that matches perfectly with the murder of . . ." There was a moment of silence punctuated by some vague background noises. "Nicholas Thompson. Last night a man near George Yard was killed by the exact same weapon."

Eric stood up again. "How was he killed?"

"Shot in the back with a nine-millimeter, the same weapon used in your case."

"Boss!" Martin Stern stuck his head in the doorway. He looked alarmed. Eric waved for him to wait, but he could tell Stern thought he was onto something big.

Once the phone call was over, the pair walked down to the video room.

"You have to see this," Martin said in an excited tone.

Stern started the video. A woman dressed entirely in black walked in through the doorway. All they could make out was one long, dark outline.

"There's a Middle Eastern family living in this building," said Stern. "At first I thought she was the boy's mother. I've seen her go in and out at least a dozen times in the footage. But then I realized that I'd already seen her go in two hours earlier, and I never saw her come out again."

"Maybe that's a friend or a relative. When does she come out again?"

Stern's eyes were sparkling with a strange light. He was sure he'd found something, and he wanted to show Eric all the little details as a buildup to his big conclusion. "Just twenty minutes later!"

The video spun forward quickly and stopped just as the same figure was coming out of the building. She was wearing large black sunglasses and holding her veil up over her mouth.

"She's hiding . . ." murmured the detective. "And that's not how Jassim dresses; she's not that . . . covered. You're right. There's something strange here. That just might be our suspect."

"But that's not it!" exclaimed Stern. They'd finally gotten to his point. "Watch this. Look carefully." He started the video back up again from the beginning. The figure who came out through the building's entrance walked down the sidewalk until she was out of the video camera's field of vision. "See anything strange?"

Eric leaned in close to the screen and motioned for Stern to play it again. He was right. There was something strange. "Her gait . . . it's extremely . . . ungainly. Uncomfortable."

"That's right. Imagine you were wearing high heels. How would you walk?" Stern's mouth spread in a smile that ran from ear to ear.

Finally Eric understood what his colleague was referring to. "It's a man . . ."

Up on the big screen in the meeting room a man was stumbling heavily down a deserted and poorly lit street. He turned around for a moment, then moved forward again. Then something startled him. The video stopped.

"This is when the first shot was fired," explained Agent Lennox. "It hit the wall to the victim's left. He collapsed here, which is where we found him." Using a laser pointer, the officer indicated a small area in the image.

"Do we see anything else?" asked Eric.

Miriam and Jane were sitting alongside him. After receiving the call from Lennox, Shaw quickly organized a meeting with the City Police so that they could gather as much information as possible about their new case.

In all likelihood the killer was the same person. The detective handling the case for City willingly handed the reins over to the investigators at Scotland Yard, offering to help in any way he could. All the evidence they'd gathered, including the ballistics reports, was turned over to Eric and his team. The body had been sent to Dr. Dawson, who would handle the autopsy. The general impression was that City had decided to wash its hands of the case. The fact that they'd sent a simple agent to meet with Eric and his team, even though it was the detective who'd handled the crime scene, was indicative of the distance City was trying to put between itself and the dead body.

On one hand this annoyed Eric, but it was also the price they had to pay in order to make sure they wouldn't wind up with someone from the union office buzzing around the department, putting pressure on everyone and harping on about the negative effects this sort of crime could have on summer tourism in the city. It could be worse. There might have been veiled criticism about how if only they'd done their jobs and caught the criminal, this second homicide would never have happened.

"Oh yes, we certainly do." Lennox started the video again.

The man being followed fell down on the ground, and a dark outline appeared in the lower left corner of the image. Everyone's eyes focused on it. The camera filmed the perpetrator from above, showing the left hand holding the pistol, then the rest of the body. It didn't make much difference, though. The figure was dressed completely in black from head to toe.

"Looks like the same person from the other video," said Miriam, who was seated at one of the tables. She was moving her legs in an agitated rhythm as if sitting on hot coals.

"Somewhat disturbing," said Jane. "Looks like Death in person." She got up and took a few steps closer to the screen, concentrating on the image while she nibbled on her enameled right index fingernail.

Eric sighed. "Could be anyone, but the clothing does look a lot alike."

From what little they could see in the black-and-white images, the killer was wearing a sort of tunic or robe that stretched all the way down to his feet, and a veil over his head. The frame never showed the killer's face, but they could see the murder weapon, which had been equipped with a silencer, just as they suspected.

The victim turned over on the ground, growing agitated. It seemed like he was saying something, but the camera was too far away for them to read his lips. Suddenly a little cloud of dust exploded alongside his right arm, and the man winced.

"That's the second shot," said Lennox. "I think he missed on purpose. He just wants the guy to get up. And in fact, here we see him stand up again."

The man struggled to his feet. The black figure took a few steps forward, moving closer to the victim.

"The shooter looks a little less clumsy than in the other video," said Jane, her eyes still glued to the big screen.

"Maybe the killer was wearing more comfortable shoes," suggested Eric.

Jane responded with a skeptic look. "Let's have Stern analyze the two videos. I'm sure he'll be able to tell us more."

Now the victim was standing up, facing the assassin. The killer made a small circle with the barrel of the pistol, and the victim turned around immediately, facing the other direction. There was a small flash from the weapon before the man collapsed on the ground.

"The killer had him turn around so that he'd be shot in the back!" Eric motioned to Lennox to stop the video, then examined the still for a few seconds.

It didn't make any sense. If the goal was simply to kill that man, why have him turn around? The modus operandi was completely different from the other killing, although in both cases the assassin had behaved unusually.

"It all seems carefully studied, choreographed, even. It almost seems like the assassin is trying to reproduce something. As if the killings are a message . . ." Eric was talking to himself as much as he was to rest of the room.

"Do you think we're dealing with a serial killer here?" said Detective Leroux. She had stopped squirming in her seat, but now she was drumming her fingers on both knees.

"I don't know." Eric shook his head, more in response to his own thoughts than to Miriam's question. "Let's move forward."

Lennox started the video again. The black figure went over to the dead victim and stooped close to the body. Then he stood up and left, walking calmly in the opposite direction from which he had come, until he disappeared from view.

"Maybe the key is to figure out the content of the message," suggested Jane.

Eric turned around and met the eyes of his second in command. "And who it's for."

FROM MINA'S BLOG

I don't know which one of the three killed Paul. Their boss chewed them out for not having left anyone alive, so it wasn't him. Maybe it was the same one who killed my mother.

No matter how hard I try, I still can't remember the order in which the yelling and the shooting took place. If I try closing my eyes to concentrate, I can see it all. It's all still there in my head, just confused, like an endless nightmare.

So I decided to kill them at random.

Today I realized for the first time what I've become: a serial killer. Maybe not in the traditional sense of the term, since one day, when my mission is over, I'll stop killing people. But I am able to enjoy the desire for destruction all the same, so maybe I am a serial killer. I feel like a predator hunting its prey—pulling it down and then tearing it apart. The feeling of supreme control this gives me is . . . intoxicating. Throughout my life I've tried to control the events taking place around me so that no one could hurt me anymore, so that nothing would ever sneak up on me and overwhelm me, but I've never felt as successful at it as I do now.

It doesn't just happen when one of those bastards is begging me or when I pull the trigger and see his life drain out of his eyes. No. It's as if, ever since I started doing this, everything around me has started to move and evolve according to a plan I created, according to my own design. I can face anything at all now because I know I'll emerge victorious.

I'm not afraid of anything, not even the people trying to stop me. I feel untouchable. Not even he can get to me.

I know I'll see it through to the end. The only fear I have now is that I might not feel as satisfied as I do now when the killing finally stops. Will this be enough? Will I thirst for more blood?

CHAPTER 8

"Oh, please, Dad!" Brian's face had turned red. "You can't ask me that." He went back to playing with his french fries, spreading them all over the plate.

"I was just asking if there's a girl at school who's more than a friend to you," Eric said with a laugh, even though his heart was filled with very real fatherly pride. He understood from the boy's reaction that he'd hit the mark. "They're reasonable questions between *men*." He wanted to make the boy feel proud, make him feel older than his fifteen years, despite Eric's hopes that he'd remain a boy for quite some time to come.

Brian scrutinized his father, apparently unconvinced. Maybe he didn't believe him, but Eric was ready to bet that Brian would like to have that kind of relationship with his father.

Ever since Eric had moved out, the way he interacted with his son had changed. He'd always been an affectionate father, but one who stood firm when needed. Though recently, he'd felt a change in his son's attitude. Brian was an adolescent now, and it seemed like the boy blamed his dad for bringing his parents' marriage to an end. To be honest, Eric blamed himself a little too, even though he continued to tell himself that his ex-wife knew full well what she was getting into—that she knew he was a man dedicated to his work, and all the more so once his career took off and he quickly became head of the scientific investigations department. Despite this, he didn't blame her for feeling abandoned, and he couldn't bring himself to be critical of his son, who was the only real victim in the situation. The problems in his relationship with Crystal had been there from the start and had gotten more acute as time went on, but Brian was the only one who couldn't possibly be to blame. With these feelings lingering, Eric had recently begun to try to change the way he approached his son, driven by the fear that the boy would merely grow further away from him.

So far he thought he was doing a good job. The positive thing was that, in a certain sense, right from the moment he and Crystal had separated, they'd begun spending more quality time together as father and son.

Of course, before, they'd lived in the same house, but that meant each took the other's company for granted a little. Now the time they spent together had become special. At least, it was for Eric, but he could feel that somehow it was for his son too, even though it was all but impossible to get the boy to admit it.

"Let's just say there might be a girl like that," said Brian, abandoning his fork altogether. Apparently he needed all his strength just to concentrate on this conversation.

"And does this *potential* girl have a name too?" asked Eric, leaning forward like somebody ready to share a secret.

"Nicole." The boy's voice trembled just a little pronouncing her name.

"Nicole," repeated his father, nodding in approval. "Let's talk about her for a moment. What's she like?"

"Blond. Tall." Brian gesticulated, practically daydreaming. "With two . . ." Here he hesitated. His hands were open, eloquent, mimicking two particularly large somethings. "Beautiful eyes," he concluded. His face flushed red.

Eric couldn't help but laugh. "Oh yes. I've always been fascinated by women's eyes too!"

Brian laughed too. In the end, they'd managed to create a nice rapport. "It's not like that, Dad. She's . . . intelligent. Very intelligent."

"I don't doubt it," said Eric, careful to look serious and thoughtful.

"She always sits at the desk next to mine during our French lessons. Sometimes she explains stuff to me that I don't understand."

Something in the tone of Brian's voice told Eric that schoolwork wasn't really the reason he was so interested in talking to this Nicole, but he preferred hearing that from Brian himself.

"You should hear the way she speaks French. It's so sexy."

Eric coughed. He'd almost inhaled his food. He wanted to be a hip, modern father, but hearing the word *sexy* come out of his son's mouth was surprising nonetheless.

"I suck at it," continued the young man, the corners of his mouth turning down in an expression that was more shame than sadness. "French might as well be Arabic for me!"

So that's why he was so frustrated. He was afraid that this girl, whom he clearly liked very much, might think he wasn't that smart.

The thought that this girl might be making his son feel this way on purpose just to get the upper hand crossed Eric's mind for a moment, but he decided to ignore it as best he could. But the idea did lead him to think of something that was supposed to be absolutely off-limits for the evening, an evening he had decided to dedicate entirely to his son by taking the boy out for dinner the way he'd been promising to do for some time now.

"Wait just a second," Eric said, another idea clicking into place. "Did you ask Miriam to help you with your French so that you could make a good impression on this girl?"

"No . . . Did she tell you? I made her promise she wouldn't tell you about that!"

They both laughed.

"How are the private lessons going?"

"I don't know." Brian picked his fork back up and grabbed a mouthful of french fries. Now that his secret was out, his appetite had come back with a vengeance. "Tomorrow I have another lesson," he said between bites. "Hopefully I'll do better than I did last time."

"I'm sure you'll surprise her."

Brian nodded. "I'm giving it all I've got!"

Pride swelled in Eric's chest. This boy, with a mouth full of fries and a daydream of a pretty girl glinting in his eyes, was the most important thing in Eric's life.

"So," said Eric, drawing everyone's attention and putting an end to the hubbub in the meeting room. "Let's try and sum everything up for a moment and focus on the facts. Then we'll worry about speculation."

He was standing beside a large screen that showed the details of the two investigations, preparing to organize the team so they could deal with what the media had already baptized the "Black Death Killings." Not exactly the world's most original name, but it stuck. Journalists were advancing a variety of different theories, including that of a serial killer, which was always a magnet for public attention, even though in this case the victims weren't exactly attracting widespread compassion.

"We have two murders, apparently different from one another." He pointed to the two photographs displayed at the top of the screen. Each showed the victim's body as it was found on the murder scene, flanked by a portrait of the victim from when he was still alive. "Nicholas Thompson, killed at home almost two weeks ago. Two shots from a nine-millimeter equipped with a silencer. One bullet to the groin, another to the neck. Both very precise shots. The bullets hit here and here, one stopping in his pelvis, the other at a vertebra. Both tore open major arteries. He died from loss of blood. The victim was a previous offender but appeared to have lived an honest life for the past fifteen years. When he was younger he was charged with a number of robberies, but none of them were particularly violent."

A few of the people in the room nodded here and there during Shaw's speech.

"Here, on the other hand, we have Gerald McKinsey. He was killed in City less than forty-eight hours ago, just before dawn, with a single shot to the back. Again, the weapon used was a nine-millimeter. The bullet entered here, perforated his lung, and entered his heart. The victim was dead just a few seconds after he hit the ground. McKinsey was a previous offender as well. He'd been in and out of prison ever since he was seventeen years old. He was last released twenty-one months ago. He too was charged with a number of robberies, including some at gunpoint." Eric paused to look around the room and let it all sink in.

"The same pistol was used for both killings," he continued. "In both cases, the victims were forced to assume a very precise position before they were killed. The first was forced to lie down, supine." He used a little laser pointer to indicate this on the screen. "The second to turn around but remain standing." The red laser dot moved to the other image. "The first body was moved, presumably because the victim was thrashing around before he died. This suggests that our assassin wanted the body to be in a certain position when it was found."

Eric stood a little to one side in order to make sure everyone could see clearly.

"Thompson let his killer in, apparently of his own free will, since he made the killer a cup of tea before he was shot. McKinsey, however, was followed. He passed through that neighborhood every day after he was done with work, though not on that street. He may have changed his route because he was attempting to escape his killer."

The laser dot moved to a black silhouette located at the middle of the screen.

"In both cases, our assassin was picked up by surveillance cameras. In the first case, while he was going into the building, and then again when he came out roughly twenty minutes later. In the second case, while he was killing his victim. He was wearing a black tunic and veil, like the kind Muslim women wear—the kind that cover the nose and mouth. However, we can't be sure both crimes were committed by the same person. Stern . . ." He turned to Martin. "What can you tell us about the two videos?"

"Ahem. Well . . ." Martin seemed surprised he'd been called on so early in the meeting. He stood up and went over to the computer connected to the big screen, opening a new image in an empty corner of the monitor. "In the first video, shot in full daylight, I analyzed the suspect's gait and body. The color of the tunic flattens the form a little, but the computer can help show us what the eye can't see. First of all, the killer is walking clumsily and seems to have a hard time with high heels. An analysis of the shadows in the image shows us that his pelvis is narrower than his shoulders. I believe we're dealing with a man. Now, in the second video"—Martin took a deep breath while he called up the next video, where the black figure could be seen coming into view in the lower left-hand corner—"the shot is really dark, and the camera angle doesn't help us much. All I can really say is that this time the assassin moves more comfortably. But as you can see here"—he froze the footage—"he's wearing sneakers. As far as the height is concerned, even taking into account the shoes, there's not much difference. We calculated everything based on the footage, and we couldn't find more than a one- or two-inch difference at most, well within the error margin for the measuring software."

"That said, how tall is our killer?" asked Eric.

"Between five foot eight and five foot nine. Taking into account some additional error due to the soles of his shoes or the way the veil is placed on his head, there might be another one-inch or one-and-a-half-inch margin. Not particularly tall for a man, but quite tall for a woman."

Jane and Miriam, both that tall, glanced at each other with a smile.

Stern seemed to have caught their expressions, because he cleared his voice and quickly added, "Well, of course there are lots of women that tall, even some taller . . ."

At that very moment, Adele walked into the meeting room and waded through her colleagues, finally sitting down toward the back.

"What a pleasure," said Eric out loud, "to have Miss Pennington grace us with her presence today."

The generally playful atmosphere that had developed around Stern's presentation turned cold in a heartbeat. Everyone's eyes turned to Adele.

"Sorry I'm late," murmured Adele, avoiding Shaw's severe frown. She shrunk a little in her seat, willing their eyes away.

"Stern," continued Eric, "what do you think? Could it be the same person?"

He nodded. "It might be, but of course we can't say for certain."

"Thank you, Stern."

The man went straight back to his seat, without hesitating a moment.

"Any relationship between the two victims?" Eric turned to Detective Leroux, who was leaning back against a wall to one side of the room. "Aside from the fact that they were both thieves?"

"Not directly." Her voice was firm. "They were never arrested together, and we don't have any proof that the two knew one another. However . . ." She paused, taking her smartphone out of her pocket. "Both were arrested at different times with a man named Christopher Garnish." She showed Eric an image of a fortysomething man.

"Garnish is a bit younger than they were," Shaw noted. The victims were both in their sixties.

Miriam nodded. "Back when he was busted with the victims he was around twenty, just getting started."

"Old news," interjected Jane. She was sitting in the front row, holding her tablet in her lap, her legs crossed. Eric's gaze was involuntarily drawn to her right ankle sticking out from the cuff of her long white slacks. She was wearing an anklet that jingled when it hit the side of her sandals as she bounced her leg up and down slightly.

"Yes, except he got a lot better," continued Detective Leroux. "So much so that he's a suspect in a number of high-profile robberies: museums, art galleries, villas . . . These have always been rumors, of course, and we've never been able to prove anything. Some people say he's just lucky. But I think most of them are made up . . . Nobody has had a confirmed sighting of him in years. He likes to stick to the shadows."

"Do we have any idea where he is right now?" asked Eric.

"We don't have any home address," said Miriam, frowning. "But I don't think he's really out-and-out hiding. After avoiding the law for this long, he must feel a little untouchable. I think we can scare him out of whatever hole he's crawled into."

"Good," Eric said, pleased. "Track him down and get him in here. It's time we had a nice little chat with Mr. Garnish. So far he's the only element that might help us shed a little more light on the motives behind these crimes."

Miriam nodded.

"Any progress with the physical evidence?" asked Eric, looking out at everyone in the room.

"Nothing noteworthy, unfortunately," said Jane. "Thompson's house was even dirtier than the street where McKinsey was killed, if you can believe that. We found a little bit of everything, but so far nothing that we can connect with the assassin. No fingerprints on the table or the door. The killer took the teacup, plate, and spoon with him when he left, so no DNA there . . . We have a partial print on the victim's shoe, but we couldn't find any fibers or anything else distinguishable from the rest of the garbage lying around that place on the clothing. As far as the other crime scene is concerned"—she ran her finger around the tablet—"we have the data the City Police provided." She nodded to Agent Lennox, who had spent the entire time sitting apart from the others, silently watching the meeting unfold. "Two bullets. One in the wall and another in the pavement, both from the same weapon. No shoe prints distinguishable from the thousands of others present there in the alley."

"So basically, we've got nothing," Eric concluded.

Jane shrugged. "That's what I've said."

"There's nothing left except to concentrate on motive and the deliberate scene the assassin took pains to create," Eric said, then went back to looking at the photographs of the victims as the rest of the team talked with one another. At first he'd thought the motive might be linked with some sex crime from the past, but the second murder had muddied the water. Yet there was something here, some sort of scheme, something familiar . . . He just couldn't quite make it out.

"Um," came Miriam's voice, rising up over the others and silencing them little by little. "The presumed rape victim from when Thompson was back in high school—well, she has a son, but he lives in Glasgow."

"Is there any chance he was in London at the same time the crimes were committed?" This trail was lukewarm at best now, and he could already imagine her answer.

"For the first date he doesn't really have a solid alibi. He says he was home alone, in Scotland, but on the second night he was on a plane, flying over the Atlantic toward New York. British Airways has confirmed he was on board. There's no way he could have been in City at the time of the murder."

"Okay, well it was worth running down just to be sure." He took a deep breath. "Aside from the mask thing, dressing all in black, which I think the killer needed in order to hide his identity, I'm guessing we're dealing with an assassin who has very precise motives. We need to figure out what those are."

"Could it be a nut job who copycats other crimes? If that's the case, we might be dealing with a serial killer." This was the second time Miriam had suggested this, and once again there was a strange light in her eyes.

"Two homicides are not enough to start talking about serial killers," protested Eric.

"It might be nice to keep him from committing a third," Miriam added, not yet ready to let it go.

"If there is a third," said Jane.

"I'm betting there will be." Miriam seemed quite sure of herself, convinced of what she was saying. There was a challenging tone in her voice as she addressed the entire room.

"At this point we can't rule anything out," said Eric. He was working to calm down everyone in the room, since people were starting to get a little too worked up. "See if you can find some similarities with any other cases."

"Good," said Miriam.

"We have to consider two possibilities: either the victims' identities are the keys to figuring out the motive, or the motive can only be identified in the killer's modus operandi," Jane said.

"What if both are important?" Adele's voice rang out from the back of the room, making everyone turn around.

"What's on your mind?" Eric said, not even trying to hide a smile.

"Vendetta!" said Adele, all but shouting the word. The colleagues closest to her started a little.

Eric said nothing for a moment, focusing on her. What was going through her mind?

"That might be the motive. Vendetta. These crimes are reconstructions, appropriate punishment for something the victims have done, not just the emulation of some psychopath."

Every single person in the room was silent, hanging on her words.

"Let's think about the murders separately for a moment and try to figure out what the assassin is trying to communicate. The pistol might simply be a symbol. We should examine unresolved cases and look for a murder where the victim was struck from behind, maybe with a knife or hand ax." She turned her head and looked outside as if searching for inspiration. "Or a victim that was castrated or, if it's a woman . . ." She lowered her head a bit. "Raped." She accompanied that word with a nod. "And then"—here Adele drew one finger across her throat—"sliced open."

Everyone in the room began talking among themselves, increasing the noise level a little.

"The same weapon," said Adele, raising her voice to be heard above the hubbub. "This whole staging and the black costume all work to make us think that we're dealing with the same assassin and therefore that the victims are somehow connected. But let's just suppose for a moment that that's not the case." She stood up. Her look and the amused curve of her lips seemed to conceal some secret that only she was privy to. "Let's imagine for a moment that two different people both killed their victims in a certain, specific manner in order to vindicate another crime. Two different people—but they know each other; they dress the same way and use the same weapon in order to make us believe that they're one and the same."

At this point it seemed like every single person in the room felt an irresistible urge to share his or her opinion, all at the same time.

"A picturesque theory," said Eric, trying to bring the room back to order, "but interesting." As often happened during those months, Pennington had managed to look at the case from a completely different point of view. She had an entirely creative approach to shuffling evidence around, which mirrored her behavior. She always sat separate from the others during these meetings, observing everything, absorbing data like a sponge before adding her two cents. Shaw expected her to chip in from one moment to the next, and when he heard her speak up, he was certain she would contribute some unusual and unexpected point of view.

"Or . . ." Adele's face darkened, as if she'd been struck by a disturbing revelation. "If our victims really are connected to one another, then the assassin might just be a single person. But in that case . . ." She stared straight at Eric, as if to send him a private message, which he picked up on just a moment before she spoke. "The murders the killer is vindicating must have taken place together."

CHAPTER 9

The key turned in the lock and the door opened.

"Eric?" said Miriam, putting one foot into the dark apartment. "You here?"

No response.

She went inside. A powerful gush of air blew past her, mussing up her hair. The door slammed shut behind her, making her jump. *"Putain!"* she swore to herself.

She walked into the living room, where the ambient light from the city softly came through the curtains. The French doors in to the balcony were still open. She walked over and pulled the curtains aside.

"There you are," she said, stepping out onto the balcony.

Eric turned around quickly, startled.

"Sorry. You weren't answering, so I used the keys."

"Hey," he said. He seemed distracted, preoccupied. Then he turned around and went back to staring out over the city.

She went over to him, leaning back against the railing so that she could look him in the eyes. "You okay?"

Eric closed his eyes for a moment and smiled a little. Then he turned to her. "Yeah, I'm all right. I'm just really tired."

Miriam took one of his arms in both her hands and shook him ever so slightly. Then she pulled in close, laying her head on his shoulder in a gesture of affection that she'd started using ever since they'd become close enough for it to be okay. "Lately you've been working too much. You should take a little time off for yourself."

Eric's face relaxed. He caressed her hair a little with his free hand. "I remember back when I was the one who gave *you* advice."

"I've grown. I'm wiser than you now."

They both laughed. Shaw freed himself from her embrace and put his arm over her shoulder, pulling her in close again so that they could look out over the city together. The pair stood there for a few moments in silence, staring at London by night.

"I'm serious, though," said Miriam. "I'm worried about you. Ever since my parents died, you're the closest thing to a father I've got."

Eric sighed. "Your aunt and uncle wouldn't be very happy to hear you say that. They're the ones who raised you, not me. They think of you as their daughter."

"I love my aunt and uncle. They've been wonderful to me. It's just that they were there before too, and I can't bring myself to see them as mother and father. With you it's different. You weren't there before, but after, you were always there for me. You've always shown me the right way, given me sound advice." She was winding one of her curls around her index finger. "You *saved* me. It's as if you took their place. If I've become who I am today—Miriam Leroux, detective with the homicide investigative unit at Scotland Yard—it's thanks to you. You've taught me everything I know about this job. You're my guide, my leader."

Eric hugged her tight but didn't say a thing. He could tell she was emotional, but she seemed to be struggling with something as well.

One small, lone tear worked its way out of the corner of her eye. She reached up and quickly wiped it away. Miriam wasn't herself either, but she couldn't stand by and say nothing. "I can see you're unhappy," she said, knowing that she had to begin somewhere. "And I want to do something to help you, just like you've done for me all these years."

"I'm okay, Miriam."

"That's not true!" she protested vehemently. "You're so . . . so *alone*!"

Eric shook his head and snorted.

"I love Crystal like a mother, and it hurt a lot when the two of you got separated, but it's been over two years since your divorce now. You have to move forward. You need to move forward."

"Don't you think I am?" he said at length, a trace of annoyance in his voice.

"No. Definitely not."

Shaw pulled away from her and placed both hands on the balcony railing.

"I understand. Do you know that?" continued Miriam. "I can understand why you're attracted to her." Even though she hadn't said Adele's name, she could see a tremor run through his body. "She's young, beautiful, intelligent, very good at her job, and plus . . . there's this *thing* between the two of you. It's really an irresistible mix, but even you must be aware that all this won't do either of you any good."

"There's nothing between me and Adele."

"Oh, yes there is."

"I know what you're referring to," Eric said, finally turning to meet Miriam's gaze. "That little scene with the key the other day. It's not what you think. Nothing happened."

"You don't have to justify yourself to me."

"You're behaving like a jealous daughter."

"I'm behaving like a concerned daughter."

"I can take care of myself, thank you."

"It doesn't seem that way—not from the way you're behaving," she exclaimed, raising her voice a little too much.

"I already told you," Eric murmured. "Nothing happened between me and Adele."

"If nothing has happened yet . . ." said Miriam, pausing. "It's because even you know that it wouldn't be right. But if you don't pull away from her, if you don't at least try to get her out of your head, sooner or later something *will* happen. And then you'll really risk getting hurt." She moved back in close to Eric, running her hand along the railing. Her bracelet tinkled a little against the metal. "I don't want you to suffer anymore."

"You don't want me to be alone; you don't want me to be with someone. What exactly am I supposed to do, according to you?"

"Oh, of course I want you to find someone. *Zut!* You're a handsome man, intelligent, witty . . . There's an army of women marching around out there who would tear each other's eyes out just to be with you. *Maybe* even someone more your age." She saw him open his mouth to protest that last jab, but she cut him off before he could. "Of course I want you to find somebody. It's just that your somebody can't be *Adele*."

"Well, if that's what you're worried about, then worry no more. It's not even an issue. She's not attracted to me at all."

Miriam burst out in sarcastic laughter and didn't make any effort to hide it. "Sure, boss!"

"And while we're on the subject," continued Eric, "why don't you tell me about you? Whatever happened to Jonathan?"

"Oh no, you're not changing the subject!"

"Come again? You get to rummage around in my private life, but I'm not allowed to ask you about yours?"

Miriam put her hands on her hips. As usual, it was all but impossible to reason with Eric. He always plowed ahead, following his own path, ignoring other people's opinions, especially hers. Despite everything she had gone through, he continued to view her as little more than a baby girl.

"So?" he said, provoking her.

And in the end she had to give in. "We're not seeing each other anymore. He was always complaining about the late nights. I couldn't take it anymore and I left him."

"Ah. That's a shame." Eric flaunted a contrite expression. "You're a beautiful girl, intelligent and witty," he said in a singsong voice. "You really should find someone."

"There's time for all that. I'm not in any hurry."

"Of course. You've got all the time in the world because you're young. You can get together and break up again whenever you want. I, on the other hand, need to settle down with someone my age before it's too late, right?"

She was hurt by the contempt in his voice. She hadn't meant to make him feel like an old man.

"Did you ever stop to think that after having been married for almost fifteen years, maybe I'd like to have a little fun?"

"And you want to have this *fun* with Adele Pennington?" she said, her voice rising.

"Why not? I know you don't like her very much, but you don't have to be that way."

That was too much. This was turning childish. "You know full well that's not the problem."

Eric gripped the railing in anger, making it vibrate. "I know, but it's still my business." He glared at her, furious, so much so that for a moment Miriam feared she'd pushed him too far. But then he turned on one heel and went back inside.

He was right. It wasn't her business.

"We'd better get going," said Eric from inside the apartment. "Jane must be wondering what's happened to us."

Miriam took one last, disconsolate look out over the dark sky. The clouds hung so low that they reflected the city light, creating a depressing reddish glow that seemed to mirror what she felt in her heart.

* * *

An unbearable cacophony of voices emerged from the pub, making it seem like the building was swelling, fit to burst. The enormous crowd inside only confirmed that impression. People were everywhere, elbowing each other for room, laughing, talking, drinking. The background music was a little loud, but even so it was impossible to tell exactly what song was playing.

While Miriam moved out into the crowd, Eric stood off to one side. He was already overwhelmed by all the different thoughts racing through his head, memories he'd thought he'd put away for good. He'd hoped that coming to this party would be a positive distraction, but now that he was here, his senses under assault from all sides, he felt even more alone and isolated than he had back home in his apartment. He would come away from this with a monster headache, just to end the day with a bang.

"Eric!" A familiar voice rose up above the others.

He craned his neck and looked around, searching for the voice's owner before finally making out Jane's contagious grin. He could only identify her by her smile, because the rest of her was unrecognizable. She didn't look at all like he was used to seeing her.

Jane was wearing a long green evening gown covered with sequins. Her usually wavy hair had been ironed flat, and it seemed longer than before. She was wearing a headband adorned with a long green feather. It was an outfit that had nothing to do with the woman he usually saw dressed in elegant silk pants and pressed white shirts when they were together in the office.

"Wow! I didn't know the circus was in town," said Eric, smiling.

She laughed merrily and then gave him an enormous hug. "Oh, Eric, I'm so happy you came!"

"Wouldn't miss it for the world," said Eric. He took a small red package with a beautiful gold ribbon out of his pocket and gave it to her. "Happy birthday!"

"Oh, you shouldn't have!" said Jane, snatching the package out of his hand. She seemed overjoyed. Given the way she was talking, Eric supposed she'd already enjoyed a few too many drinks. But that was fine. After all, it was her birthday and she deserved it.

Jane, wearing long, white silk gloves, had a little difficulty opening the gift. After loosening the ribbon, she unwrapped a pair of lacquered steel earrings—all the latest rage, or at least that's what the jewelry saleswoman had told him.

"They're fantastic! Thanks, boss." She planted a big kiss on his cheek.

"You're having a banner night, aren't you?" said Eric, rolling his chin to take in the entire room. "I hope nobody calls the cops for an emergency tonight. Things could get embarrassing," he added with a grimace.

His comment only made Jane laugh harder. "Impossible! I invited the entire Scotland Yard!"

"There we go. Now it all makes sense."

"We'll do it again in September when it's your birthday. It'll be great!" Waving her arms around in excitement, Jane accidentally struck a passing waiter in the face. "Oh, I'm sorry," she said before grabbing a couple of glasses off the waiter's tray.

"To tell you the truth," said Eric, "I was planning on doing something a little more low key."

"No, no, no . . ." Jane offered him one of the glasses, filled to the brim with an unknown liquor. "You only turn fifty once. You have to exaggerate."

He looked sidelong at his second in command, throwing her an ironic smile before eventually accepting the drink. "Well, don't get your hopes up. I'm certainly not wearing anything like that!" He gestured to his colleague's outfit. Jane, her drink on her lips, started laughing so hard she practically choked on it. Eric start laughing too, but he studied his drink a little more carefully before imbibing. The last time he'd had something to drink when he didn't know what it was, the evening hadn't exactly been a success.

"Did you come with Miriam?" asked Jane, shaking her dress a little where her drink had spilled on it. She wiped it clean with the back of her hand that held the gift. Fortunately the cloth was resistant and she cleaned it off before the fabric absorbed so much as a drop.

"Yes, but I lost her in the crowd." He craned his neck and looked around briefly to see if he could find his "adopted" daughter nearby. "The last time I saw her she was looking for the bar."

"Oh, that's sweet. Instead of me, she's looking for the bar." Jane laughed again. This time Eric didn't imitate her.

"Did something happen?" His second in command had a sixth sense for trouble, and apparently it worked even when she was a few sheets to the wind.

He waved his hand, minimizing it. "Nothing, nothing. You know how Miriam can be."

Jane made a sound of agreement, but she seemed to be nodding to what Eric *hadn't* said. "In any case," she said, giving him an allusive smile, "Adele's already here, if you're interested."

Eric shot her a reproving look, even though he found himself fighting off the impulse to start looking around immediately for the other woman.

"All right," said Jane, throwing back what was left of her drink and plopping the glass down on a table where a few of their colleagues were hotly discussing some topic. "I need a mirror so that I can try out my new present!" She held up the little red box with the earrings and shook it. "You go ahead and mingle. Eat something. Have a drink. Have fun, Eric. That's what I'm saying!" She gave him a pat on the shoulder and turned away.

Eric, still smiling, focused on the drink he was holding in one hand. Sure, why not? He took a sip, and almost instantly his mouth was on fire. He swallowed, and his entire esophagus went up in flames. The heat radiated, expanding in his stomach as his face twisted against the burn.

Better to move around a little. His eyes still watering, he located a table he could abandon his drink on so that he wouldn't be tempted to have another sip. He wiped one hand across his forehead, where a light sweat had broken out, and took a deep breath.

In doing so, he made something out on the other side of the room. Something feminine. Adele.

She was leaning against the wall, apparently alone. She watched the party and took occasional sips of her beer. When a couple of reckless dancers lost their balance and collapsed at her feet, she laughed along with the rest of the crowd.

Then, suddenly, she turned her gaze toward Eric and their eyes met.

Adele flashed one of her enigmatic smiles and lifted her mug to toast him. Then her expression changed and she looked a little more perplexed. She felt at her side with a free hand, located her purse, and then dug around in it until she found her smartphone. She concentrated on the screen for a moment. After that she moved, disappearing from Eric's view while he looked around, trying to figure out where she'd gone.

Without thinking about it, Eric elbowed his way through the crowd, trying to catch up with Adele.

He went out through a back door into an alley behind the bar. It was empty. As soon as the door closed behind him, the noisy hubbub from the party was squelched into a faint, muffled roar, as if they were celebrating far away.

Eric walked down the three stairs that brought him to street level but wound up with one foot in a deep puddle. It must have rained during the short time he'd been inside. A streetlight shone directly overhead, and everything illuminated in its cone of light glistened with a wet sheen. It had been a short, intense summer shower.

The air felt fresher, or maybe that was just the shift in temperature. He rubbed his hands against his arms to warm up. What was he doing out here? There was nobody here but him.

"Jesus, Danny, don't be so *hysterical*." Eric spun around, searching for the source of that voice. The walls of the nearby buildings were close, echoing the voice back and forth. It could have come from anywhere, but not too far away.

Adele laughed, and Eric followed the sound.

He walked stealthily, following the wall. Farther up the alley it turned to the right, circling the pub.

A sudden cry. Quick footsteps.

Eric froze for a moment; then he ran toward the corner where the alley turned.

"Oh, sweetheart, I think you and I have a few things to say to each other," murmured a male voice.

Instinctively, Eric's right hand reached for the pistol at his side, but it wasn't there. He was off duty and hadn't brought it with him. "Fuck."

He leaned around the corner. The light was dim farther on, but he could just make out the shadow of a man who was holding Adele in a headlock, forcing her to bend over to one side. With his other arm he was holding a gun to her head. Adele had her hands in the air with her back turned to Eric. On the ground halfway between them was her smartphone, the screen still glowing.

"You're a little whore, you know that?" the man said.

Adele let out a little stifled moan but didn't answer. Another woman would have been begging, imploring the man not to hurt her. She, on the other hand, seemed to be keeping her cool.

"Now we're going to go take a little walk, you and I," said her aggressor, tightening his grip.

Eric had to do something, anything. Against all logic, he stepped out from around the corner. "Police!" he shouted as if he had his pistol ready. "Let her go!"

The man turned his head in Eric's direction but stopped halfway and glanced up overhead. The light. He shoved Adele violently to the ground and ran away.

Eric's heart stopped for a moment, then began racing faster than before.

He was at her side in an instant. "Are you okay?" He knelt down beside her and brushed her hair out of her eyes.

Adele seemed disoriented. Then her expression hardened. "I think so . . ." she said, but Eric could hear pain in her voice.

"Can you get up?"

She nodded, and Eric helped her to her feet. "Oh fuck!" said Adele. "I broke a heel!" On her feet, it was hard for her to keep her balance.

"Are you sure nothing's broken?" It hurt to see her like this, fragile, her hair and clothes dirtied with mud. She had an abrasion on one knee. He felt a compelling need to protect her but at the same time wasn't sure what he was supposed to do, or even what he was allowed to do.

Adele patted her clothing as if searching for something. "He stole my cell phone." Oddly, it seemed like her phone and her shoes were the only things she was worried about. It wasn't exactly what you'd expect from a normal victim of aggression, but then again, Adele Pennington was anything but normal.

"No, it's over there." He pointed back at the alley, and she immediately went over to pick it up. He followed her, worried. Maybe she was in a state of shock.

Adele retrieved the cell phone. She rubbed it with a clean corner of her shirt, making sure the screen wasn't broken. "He put his hands on me," she said with a grunt of disgust.

"Hey," said Eric, walking over to her and lifting her head up delicately. His fingers were under her chin so that he could look her in the eye. The weak lamplight shone on her face. Her eyes were clear, trusting. Adele swallowed and her lips trembled a little, attracting his attention.

And then, before he could stop himself, Eric bent down and kissed her.

At first she didn't move. Then she opened her mouth a little, but she didn't respond to his kiss in any other way.

The impulse, born of a desire he'd been repressing for a long time, quickly turned to guilt. In a sober flash, he pulled away from her. Adele stared up at him, a look of astonishment on her face.

What on earth was he thinking? Someone had just attacked this woman, and the best he could come up with was to take advantage of her the moment her defenses were down?

He stumbled backward a couple of steps. "I'm sorry," he murmured. "I don't know what came over me." Then he turned away, ashamed.

"It's okay," she said behind him.

Oh no, it wasn't. "I'm mortified. Please excuse me." Eric couldn't even bring himself to meet her eyes as he said it.

"Really," she insisted. "It doesn't matter."

He could hear her moving, so he started walking. He couldn't stand to be close to her. He just wanted to get away.

"Eric!" Adele's voice echoed down the alley.

He stopped. It was the first time she'd ever called him by his name. She had no idea what hearing his name come out of her mouth did to him.

A moment later her hand was on his shoulder, and a moment after that she was standing in front of him. She didn't seem scared anymore, or in shock. She was the same old Adele, breathtakingly beautiful and tough as nails. Sure of herself.

A drop of rain fell on her face, then another. Eric felt rain on his hair as he watched it wet her face, falling harder and harder. Thunder rumbled across the sky above them. Lightning flashed.

Adele smiled and raised herself up on her tiptoes, her mouth open, as rainwater poured down on them both. She began laughing, and he did too. He'd moved from desire to guilt and then to this unusual sensation, at once pleasurable and comforting. Whatever was happening, whatever this was, he never wanted it to stop.

When Adele stepped back, their eyes met. Both were still smiling. Their clothing was soaked, but who cared?

He put his hands on her sides, and she put hers on his face. A tingle of desire, indistinguishable from the electricity already in the air. Finally their mouths met in a long, passionate kiss as a downpour thundered all around them, isolating the couple from the rest of the world.

For a little while time seemed to have lost all meaning. Then, once they were both out of breath, they pulled apart and stared into each other's eyes.

Not long after that the rain began to peter out, and as it lessened, the sense of completeness that had filled Eric's heart began to diminish, as did the smile on Adele's face. The rain stopped altogether.

It was as if an enchantment had been broken. The couple pulled apart, disconcerted. They looked silently at one another for a few moments, before Adele looked away. "I think it would be better if I went home."

A deep sense of disappointment threaded its way through Eric's heart. No. He didn't want her to leave. Maybe he should offer to give her a lift? But he didn't have his car. What the hell was he thinking? He was what she was trying to get away from. He could see her regretting what had just taken place between them.

Adele took another step backward and began digging frantically in her purse. She removed her keys and, without even looking at him one last time, nodded over her shoulder, back toward the pub. She moved her lips slightly, like she was searching for the right thing to say, but in the end just murmured, "Good night." She took off as if escaping.

He watched her go, wanting nothing more than to stop her, but he couldn't say a thing. He stood there, immobile, until he couldn't see her anymore. He heard the distant noise of an engine starting up, roaring, and then a car taking off with a screech of rubber. Only then did Eric move again.

He made his way back to the pub, but the last thing he wanted to do was go inside and celebrate.

Reluctant, he went inside and was immediately met with the happy roar of the crowd. It seemed like he'd been gone for hours. He'd tell Miriam he wasn't feeling well and take a taxi back to the apartment.

"Hey, boss!" Martin Stern appeared at his side. "I didn't see you come in." This was a vaguely drunken version of Stern. He was unquestionably more carefree than usual, but that made him no less annoying to Eric at the moment. "You're all wet. What the heck happened?"

Eric skewered Martin with an icy stare, and his colleague reacted as usual, despite the alcohol, by lowering his head in submission. "See you around, b-boss," he stammered before disappearing into the crowd.

"Detective Shaw?" A man's voice rose above the hubbub.

Eric turned around to see who was calling him.

"Right here, Detective." A hand waved above people's heads. Gavin Lennox's face was beneath it. A group of people passed nearby, pushing him to one side, but Lennox kept coming toward him.

"You're here too," said Eric. It was half-question and half-statement. Jane really had invited all of Scotland Yard. At this point he wouldn't be surprised to see the mayor's head pop out from the other room.

"I was looking for you." Now the two men were standing in front of one another, and Lennox could talk in a normal tone of voice.

Shaw's brow furrowed. What the hell did this guy want now?

"Detective Leroux had to take off for . . . something urgent." Lennox made a gesture. "She couldn't find you anywhere, and she asked me to let you know."

"Miriam's already left?" It was a rhetorical question. What he really wanted to say was, *Why the fuck did she take off like that?*

Lennox shrugged. "I don't know why. We were talking, sort of. And at a certain point she glanced at her watch, then took off like a jackrabbit."

CHAPTER 10

He grabbed his kit out of the trunk and handed another to Jane, and the two detectives headed for the entrance to the small house. That morning the sun had finally decided to break free of its cloud cage, and even though it was only ten in the morning, the day was already starting to heat up.

Eric sighed. He wished he could take his jacket off. "Are you sure this is the right address?" he asked, turning to look at his colleague. It was too calm. Where were the other squad cars?

Detective Hall nodded yes. That's when he saw a uniformed policeman step out of the garden.

"Detectives," said Agent Mills. "We're all back here, on the other side. The crime scene is in the garage."

"Okay. Lead the way."

The man's face was distraught. "I'd better warn you—it's not a pretty sight."

They followed the officer across the lawn. Once they'd passed a row of hedges, they could finally see the squad cars, all their lights still on and flashing, as well as the coroner's van parked along the sidewalk. They rounded a corner and found themselves in front of the garage, its door stuck halfway open. They could see the legs of people walking around inside.

At that very moment Miriam bent down and came out of the garage, white as a sheet. She walked quickly, then started running, toward the little street. She threw a glance toward them but didn't stop.

"What's up with her?" asked Jane, turning to watch her go and practically running into Eric.

"No idea."

Once she reached the street, Miriam bent over and vomited.

"I'll be back in a moment," said Eric, alarmed. "You go on ahead." He ran over to Detective Leroux.

Miriam was steadying herself with one hand on the back of a car. She heaved, trying to vomit again, but nothing came out except a little bile.

"Hey, Miriam, are you okay?" Shaw handed her a tissue. He'd never seen her get sick at a crime scene before.

"Better than the guy in there, that's for sure," she responded, wrinkling her lips. She took the tissue and wiped her mouth.

Eric sighed. The day was off to a marvelous start.

"I feel like shit . . . ," said Miriam in a low voice. She seemed angry with herself for her reaction. Or maybe she was feeling bad about something else?

"What happened to you last night?"

Miriam rolled her eyes and smoothed her hair. She didn't seem in the mood to make conversation. "I had something to do."

"What? And it popped into your head in the middle of the party?" He wasn't really angry with her for having abandoned him the night before, even though she'd insisted on taking him. He wasn't used to this kind of behavior from her, though. He was angry, but not with her.

"Jonathan called." She waved her hand as if she wanted that to be the end of it, for that vague explanation to finish the conversation.

"Jonathan called you?" Eric said with an inquisitive tone. "Lennox told me that you glanced at your watch, then practically sprinted out of the pub. He didn't say anything about a phone call."

"What is this," she demanded, annoyed, "an interrogation?"

Eric looked at her, saying nothing. He was waiting for an answer, and she knew it.

"He called me five minutes before that, and I told him to go fuck himself . . . Then I regretted it, okay?"

"How did it go?" he asked. Every time they talked about Jonathan, he wound up cutting her off. Who knew why? At this point, he was just curious.

"Oh, forget about it." She made a grimace of denial. She wouldn't say anything more about it. "I'm going to go ask the neighbors some questions. Have fun in there," she said before walking away.

Eric could tell she was hiding something from him. She was nervous, preoccupied, but as long as she refused to talk to him about it, there was little he could do to help her.

Reluctantly Eric walked back to the garage. In order to get inside, he had to slide his kit under the door first, then bend over and scoot beneath the garage door.

What he saw when he straightened back up chilled the detective to the bone.

For a few brief moments horrible images from the past bubbled up in his mind and were superimposed on what he now found himself facing. Eric released a long, pent-up breath.

"Eric," said Dr. Dawson by way of hello. He was kneeling in front of the chair the victim's body was in—what was left of the victim's body, at least.

A flash lit up the garage, blinding Eric for a moment and shocking him out of the stupor he'd slipped into. He blinked furiously. Once he could see clearly again, he realized Adele was there, circling the cadaver and taking pictures.

The body was misshapen and covered with blood. There was a bullet hole in the back of the head. The victim had been bound at the wrists and ankles, with another rope wrapped around his chest, strapping him into the chair and preventing him from falling forward. Jane was collecting the fingerprints spread out across the floor one by one with a portable tool.

"The house and the car both belong to a man named Tom Ridley, director of an art gallery downtown." Mills was talking quietly, his gaze pointed at the wall. "Sixty-two, a widower, no children. We're trying to track down a relative who can identify the body, unless we get something from the prints."

Eric couldn't stop staring at the corpse. He found it magnetic. "What else do we know about this Ridley?" He realized he was hyperventilating. He needed to calm down, immediately. "Does he have any priors?"

Agent Mills shook his head. "Nothing, not even a parking ticket. He's clean."

"You said he ran an art gallery," said Jane. She had finished collecting fingerprints and was now loading the data into their server so that it could be forwarded to IDENT1. "Maybe he had something valuable in the house, or here in the garage." She turned to look at the shelving—dusty but empty. "Did you see if there were any signs of robbery in the house?"

"Nothing obvious."

"If it's a robbery, it took a decidedly wrong turn," said Dr. Dawson.

Hearing those words, Eric felt a wave of nausea rise up inside him. No, it couldn't be true. Couldn't be.

Another flash. Adele stepped in front of him and knelt down to photograph the hands.

"They chopped off his fingers with one clean blow. Likely with that," said the doctor, pointing to a small bloody cleaver lying on the floor. "Given the amount of blood here, I'd say he was still alive while they were torturing him. And then . . ." The doctor stood up and reached out to the victim's head with his latex-gloved hands, turning it a little. "They struck him repeatedly in the head with a blunt instrument." He examined the wounds more closely, then used a pair of tweezers to pluck some wood fiber from one of them, tucking it into a little plastic bag.

"There are medium-velocity blood sprays in almost every direction," said Jane. "He was struck repeatedly, over and over again, from different directions and just kept on bleeding."

Adele took a picture of the floor where he colleague was pointing. Backing up, she bumped Eric's arm for a brief moment, and their eyes met. He opened his mouth to say something, even though he had no idea what, but she turned away before he had the chance.

"Finally they shot him in the head," concluded Dawson. "But you'll have to wait for the autopsy before I can get the bullet."

Shaw nodded slightly, still in shock. Deep in his heart he already knew what kind of weapon the killer had used. Now he understood that strange sense of familiarity he'd felt the day before during the meeting. The images of the three victims' bodies marched through his mind, one after the other, followed by a little girl's frightened eyes.

FROM MINA'S BLOG

This time it was harder. When you pull a trigger and the other person dies, it almost seems like a game. You can fool yourself into thinking that it is a game, just to keep from realizing that you're taking a life away. The second time it was simply fun. The hunt, chasing down the prey. But Ridley's death took a long time—too long. All that blood kept coming out and coming out, pumped by a stubborn heart that just wouldn't give up.

At first he didn't understand what was happening. He truly believed he was being robbed. He stayed calm and told me to take whatever I wanted, never thinking that I might be something more than a simple thief. He didn't realize I was there for him.

After I tied him up in the chair, he started to feel afraid—I could practically smell the fear on him. Then he saw the knife and heard my name, and suddenly he realized what was in store for him. He wasn't coming out alive, not after he knew who I was, and it wouldn't be over for a long time yet.

His calm vanished in an instant. The monster turned into a weeping, whining baby. He didn't display even an ounce of the dignity my father had shown when he was in the same situation.

He would have sold his own children in the blink of an eye to save himself—if he'd had any, that is. He begged me, even when he knew it was no use.

He fainted away each time I amputated something. I had to shake him back awake so that he wouldn't sleep through the next one.

By the time I was done with the hands, he'd become completely hysterical. He kept screaming like he was possessed, even though I yelled at him to stop, telling him I'd make it last a lot longer if he didn't. He wasn't listening to me anymore. I grabbed one of the logs stacked against the wall and started whacking him in the head with it. Bright-red stains spread all over the floor, the walls, my clothing. I even felt that viscous liquid squirt onto my face. He begged me to get it over with and kill him, but I kept going, over and over again, until all my strength was gone. He was immobile, but his blood kept pumping out, along with bits of brain.

Suddenly his entire body seized with convulsions.

"Stop it! Stop it!" I shouted at him, as if he could hear me, as if he could obey me.

I was gripped with an extremely powerful wave of nausea and became afraid I might vomit from one moment to the next. I pulled out the pistol and shot him in the head. Then everything stopped.

CHAPTER 11

"I need to see the files from an old case for an investigation currently underway," said Eric, flashing his badge to the agent who oversaw access to the Metropolitan Police archives.

The woman gave him a distracted smile, barely raising her eyes from her computer screen. It seemed like she'd been interrupted during some very important task, like posting her thoughts on the meaning of life to a social network. At this hour the department was half empty. Everyone was out on lunch break, and she probably hadn't been expecting a visitor. She absentmindedly grabbed the sign-in sheet and put it on the counter in front of him. "Just write down your badge number and sign here."

Eric looked around for a pen. He was about to ask her for one, but she anticipated the question and waved one in front of his face.

"Thanks."

He was filling out the registration form when he heard the lock click and the door open in front of him.

Eric wandered through the dusty shelves. Evidence from cases that had been closed were stored for many years in these archives, filling up most of the space available in that enormous storage area. Then there were cases that were still open, cases with no deadline other than the statute of limitations. But there was no statute of limitations on a triple homicide, not even after twenty years. He worked his way back in time until he reached 1994.

The moment he recognized the big box of evidence from that massacre, Eric couldn't help but hesitate. He wasn't sure he wanted to reopen that door.

He climbed up the shelving, one row after the next, until he'd gone high enough to get what he needed. Then he brought everything down and set it on a table that stood to one side near the wall. He tried to keep his breathing calm, glancing around every once in a while to make sure no one else was there. Finally he lifted the cover.

Inside lay a series of catalogued objects, some in sealed paper envelopes, others in transparent plastic bags. These included the bloody clothing that had been worn by the victims: the woman's nightshirt, the child's pajamas, the man's sweat suit. There was even the long piece of rope the man had been tied up with.

If they were to repeat their analysis today, using the more accurate methods they'd developed in the time since, who knew whether they'd be able to identify something that had been invisible to them back then—whether they'd be able to find something that had escaped them in the past and come closer to identifying those responsible.

At the time, it had been the first truly cruel case he'd come across in his short career. He'd been twenty-nine, so he wasn't exactly a novice criminologist, but he could still remember the impression it made on him. A family destroyed in the blink of an eye. Only the little girl had survived, and only then because nobody had realized she was there.

The eyes of that little girl, sparkling in the darkness beneath that bed when he shined his flashlight on them, were like a defenseless kitten. Those eyes and the terrorized expression on her face had stayed with him for a long time. So had the smile she gave once they were outside the house, when she decided to tell him her name, the name her family called her by.

What was left of that little girl today? What was left in the woman who still bore those same eyes?

Chasing that thought out of his head, Eric took a file from the bottom of the box and then quickly closed the lid.

He decided to wait until that evening to open the file. He didn't have the courage to look at it in the office. He'd rather wait and go through it in the peace and quiet of his own home.

Once he was home, he abandoned the file on the desk in his study and did nothing more with it for a few hours, save passing by the doorway to glance at the folder from a distance. He was putting off the inevitable, but when he had no more excuses, nothing left to do in the meantime, he sat down at his desk and opened it.

The first thing he saw were the photographs of Mina's father's body, bound to a chair in the living room with his arms, legs, and torso tied to the wood. The fingers on both his hands had been chopped off. All his teeth had been knocked out. They'd struck him in the face over and over again with a golf club they'd found in the house. Then they'd carved out his eyes and shattered his skull, leaving him to die.

The similarities with what he'd seen that morning in the garage were remarkable, although the recent murderer had done less damage to the body. For that reason he couldn't be absolutely sure the killer was copycatting this homicide, even though the victim had been tied up in exactly the same way.

Then there was a photograph of the little boy. They'd shot him in the back as he was trying to get away. The murder that had taken place on the street in City a few days ago looked just like what happened to Paul. Of course, here the similarities were less marked, less obvious. Lots of people are killed that way, but whoever shot Gerald McKinsey had forced him to stand up and turn around. If his intent was merely to kill the man, why go to all the trouble? Why stage every element down to the last detail? The symbolic significance was obvious.

Finally Eric got to the photographs of the mother. He had been the one who found her on the bed. They had raped her, then cut her throat. Comparing that killing to the Thompson case—where the victim had been shot in the groin and then in the neck while sitting down—might seem forced if taken alone, but placing all three cases together, the overarching scheme was perfectly clear.

The only survivor had been the little girl. She'd survived by hiding underneath the same bed her mother was killed on. There was little doubt she'd witnessed her mother's murder. She may have seen the others take place too.

Eric paged through the file until he found the photograph he was looking for. She looked just like he remembered her, but what did she remember of that day? It was hard to say . . .

She'd been just seven years old, old enough to understand. Most of all, old enough not to forget—not completely, anyway. It was impossible to believe that the experience hadn't had repercussions on her life. Looking at her today, she seemed normal—a normal woman. No one would suspect that she'd experienced such a traumatic event in the past.

But he knew. And he was certain that she'd noticed the similarities too. What bothered him the most was that she hadn't said anything to him about it.

Suddenly Eric jumped up from his desk, driven by a wave of terror, and brought both hands to his face.

The thought that she might be involved in these crimes had just entered his mind for the first time. He struggled to drive it away with all the strength he could muster. He couldn't, wouldn't accept that.

He forced himself to breathe, in and out, in and out. He struggled to calm himself down. Losing control now wouldn't help him get to the truth.

* * *

Detective Shaw went to the refrigerator and got a beer, then stopped to sip it slowly in front of the window. The sun was about to set on that last Saturday in June. He hadn't come home this early in months. He wasn't accustomed to seeing his apartment in the light of day. It seemed different, alien somehow.

Reluctantly, he went back to his desk, where the photograph of little Mina was waiting patiently for his return. For twenty years she'd waited in vain for justice to be done.

It had been a miracle to find her alive. When they were investigating the case, they'd assumed the killers hadn't known she was there. Her bedroom was in the attic. Presumably they hadn't even seen it, so nobody knew to look for her.

This confirmed the theory that the killers didn't know the family very well.

Nobody knew them well, in truth. They'd moved to London less than a year earlier, and even their neighbors considered them mysterious. Apparently they were very reserved.

The motive for the break-in had been robbery. The house had been cleaned out; everything of value was gone. At first they couldn't figure out why the killers had been so savage with the man. Then the will was opened, revealing the presence of a small, secret safe in the attic. It was full of antique jewelry, which had been the prize for the thieves. The real mystery was how they'd come to know the jewelry even existed.

The investigative team surmised that the jewelry owner had had the pieces appraised, though no leads panned out to anything concrete, in part because they couldn't find any foreign fingerprints in the house. There were no witnesses, no surveillance system, no video cameras. None of the physical evidence provided anything that investigators could consider a viable lead.

Who knew if things would be different today, with all the new techniques that had developed since then.

The clear parallels between that case and the cases they were currently handling might be enough to justify ulterior analysis of the evidence, but Eric wasn't at all sure he wanted to reveal his discovery. Not yet.

He resumed paging through the file. He had a clear sensation that there might be something useful in there, somewhere. At a certain point his eye was drawn to a name, a name that had arisen during one of the numerous interviews they'd conducted for the investigations.

Christopher Garnish.

A satisfied smile crept across his face, followed by the sense of contained excitement he always felt whenever an important piece of evidence had been unearthed.

Garnish had been about twenty years old when they'd conducted the investigation. Something of a hell-raiser, he was the dissolute son of an auction-house owner. His father had forced him to get a job in the hope that work would help pull his son off the streets, and so Garnish had started working as a gardener, one of the few things he appeared to be good at. He'd been interrogated by the detective assigned to the case, since he was working in the garden of a house near the home where the crimes had taken place. The investigators believed Garnish might have learned about the jewelry through his father's auction house. Maybe the victim had gone there to have the jewelry evaluated.

It was a weak lead, one that eventually dissolved when they found nothing they could back it up with. They couldn't connect Garnish with anything inside the house, and in any case he appeared to have an ironclad alibi provided by his father for the night the crimes took place.

Eric closed his fingers into a fist, then stretched them open again. The fact that this name had reappeared in both the Thompson and the McKinsey cases couldn't possibly be a coincidence.

He picked up his phone and made a call. "Mills," said the voice on the other end.

"I need you to check something for me," said Eric, getting straight to the point.

"Detective Shaw!" The agent was surprised, perhaps because it was relatively rare for the chief of the scientific investigations department to call him, especially at that hour. Mills usually turned to his superior in the homicide investigations team, Detective Leroux. "Of course, sir, what do you need?"

"The Ridley case. Any connections between him and Christopher Garnish?"

Mills hesitated for a moment. "Do you think he's got something to do with the Black Death Killings?"

Eric sighed impatiently. Why couldn't people just do their jobs? "Let's call it an intuition. Could you check on that for me please?"

"Um, sure, of course." He could hear that Mills was hesitant. "Am I supposed to tell Leroux about it?"

"No, Leroux already has enough on her plate. Report to me directly." There was the peremptory tone of an order in Shaw's voice.

Of course he could have investigated this aspect himself, but that would use up valuable time. Mills would be much faster than he was in that kind of investigation.

"Okay . . ."

Eric's request was a little unusual, but Eric knew his agent. Mills would be discreet. "Thanks," he said, then hung up.

Forgetting about the telephone he was still holding in one hand, Eric went back to carefully reading through the transcription of the Garnish interrogation.

His doorbell rang, dragging him only partially back to reality.

Still lost in his thoughts, Eric walked over to the front door and opened it.

"Hi," said Adele, giving him a timid smile. "Am I bothering you?" Her eyes moved to the cordless telephone still in his hand.

Finding her here, standing before him, was the last thing Eric had expected, and he fumbled a little before regaining his composure. "How did you get into the building?" he asked.

"Oh, I'm fine, thanks, and you?" said Adele ironically.

Only then did Eric realize how brusque he was being. "Hi. Hello. I'm sorry."

"All I had to do was flash a badge to one of your neighbors and he held the door for me."

"I should have guessed," he said.

Adele took a quick look to either side of the hall, then asked Eric again, "Can I come in?"

He shook his head, silently chastising himself. The shock of finding her standing outside his door had made him forget his manners. "Of course," he said, stepping to one side to let her in. He put the phone down on the little table by the door.

Adele walked in a little hesitantly, while Shaw closed the door behind her and tried not to stumble over her.

"Please, make yourself at home," he said, pointing to the living room. He immediately thought of the file, the contents of which were spread out all over his desk.

He darted past her in order to get to file, arriving just in time to slip all the documents and photographs back into the folder and turn it over so that she couldn't see the front, which listed all the names and relevant dates in the case. When he turned around, Adele was right behind him.

"I see you've brought your work home," she said, casting an eye on the table. Eric stepped in front of her, hiding the file behind him.

"No, no, it's nothing," he said. His tone of voice was anything but convincing, but then Adele had no business nosing any further into the way he spent his free time. "I was just reviewing an old case for a court deposition," he added. There. If he focused his mind, at least he was still capable of saying something half-intelligent.

Eric took a deep breath. Why was he so nervous? A little voice inside his head suggested that he was still discombobulated by their close encounter the previous evening, but he silenced it. He was still angry about the way she'd run off, leaving him there. That thought was enough to settle him again, sweeping away the surprise he still felt at finding Adele outside his door.

"May I ask why you're here?" Now his voice was serious, resolute.

Adele sighed and cast a look around the room, as if the answer to his question were hiding somewhere within these walls. Then she looked back at him. "I thought we should talk," she said, looking him up and down.

Eric waited, determined to keep his cool and hear what she had to say.

When Eric said nothing, Adele spoke up again. "I thought about calling you, but then I decided to come so that we could talk face to face. I took a walk first in order to clear my head."

"Did it work?" he asked. He couldn't help but let a little sarcasm sneak into his voice, but Adele appeared not to hear it. Either that or she chose to ignore it.

"I think so." She was calm. Unlike Eric, she didn't appear interested in arguing. She'd already made her decision. "I think it would be best if we stop things here for a moment."

Eric half-closed his eyes, making an active effort to keep from saying what he was feeling. Her flight the night before left little room for error. In his heart he hoped she regretted that move, and her presence here in front of him had let him hope for a moment that that might be the case. In reality, he'd come to know her quite well over the past few months. She wasn't the kind of woman to let something lie, hoping that it would be forgotten over time. She wanted to end what she'd started somehow, and to make sure he understood her position. Now she was clearly telling him that what had happened between the two of them couldn't happen again.

"Good," said Shaw. He couldn't think of anything better to say. His brain was racing a hundred miles an hour, trying to come up with a decent argument on his own behalf.

Adele looked perplexed, apparently surprised to find him so docile and compliant. "Good," she repeated, sounding uncertain. She lowered her gaze and stepped back.

"Good my ass!" he burst out, making her start. "Whatever god-damn game you're playing, you need to stop. Right now!"

"I don't know what you're talking about," said Adele, defensive.

"I'm talking about your little cat-and-mouse game, the one we've been playing for weeks now." He stepped in closer, threateningly. "Except that I still haven't figured out which one of us is the cat and which one the mouse."

In that moment, and just for a fraction of a second, a look of triumph ran across Adele's face, but it disappeared so quickly that Eric doubted he'd really seen it in the first place. This was followed by a contrite, almost exasperated air. "Eric . . . ," said Adele.

God, he loved it when she called him by his name.

"I'm not saying I'm not attracted to you. You know I am," she said before pausing. She was silent for a moment, her fingers moving at her sides. Her eyes were wet. "Please don't make things more difficult than they already are."

Faced with her sudden change in direction, Shaw found himself doing the same. It would be worse if they started fighting again. "You're right. There are a million reasons why a relationship between the two of us would be rather . . . *inconvenient*."

Adele laughed then, even as a tear threaded its way down one cheek.

Eric laughed too. What the hell was he saying? It should come as no surprise if she thought he was too old for her. He was talking like an old man! But all it took was that one stupid word to lighten the mood as if by magic. "What I really want to say is—"

Adele interrupted him. "I know," she said.

"What I really want to do is make things easier."

"I know."

"Then what do you want me to do?"

Adele leaned her face in to his, moving to one side and bringing her mouth close to his ear. "Stop for just a moment," she whispered clearly. Then she planted a chaste kiss on his cheek.

Eric stood there, his mouth open, as all the possible meanings of those five words chased each other in circles in his head.

Adele drew back and sighed, reacquiring at least a little of her self-control. "See you around," she said, backing up. Then she turned around and was gone.

CHAPTER 12

He carefully set the bullet that had been removed from Ridley's head beneath the microscope. The laboratory was silent, as was to be expected at eight o'clock on a Sunday morning. The morning team hadn't even come in yet. This was always the best time to analyze ballistics without attracting any undue attention.

Usually Eric concentrated on being the boss, leaving the small tasks to the other criminologists, but every once in a while he enjoyed slipping on a lab coat and picking up the tools of his trade, especially after they'd acquired some new instruments. He enjoyed staying up to date and was careful not to find himself relying too much on the people who worked around him, especially when there were special circumstances in play.

The things he was dealing with today unquestionably fell into this last category.

He put an image of the bullet up on the screen. All the characteristic lines and streaks left by its high-velocity voyage down the barrel of the gun were clear and in focus. Then he called up the findings from the McKinsey murder in the database. The computer took just a few seconds to analyze the data, but he didn't have to wait until the word

Corresponds popped up on the screen in order to see he was right. It was obvious even to the naked eye.

For a moment he'd hoped this wouldn't be the case. It would mean he'd been wrong from the start. It would have been better if it weren't true, even though that would mean he had an entirely new case to resolve. But it was true. It was the same case. The man dressed in black, the Black Death, had struck again.

"Find a match?"

Eric jumped a little when he heard Jane's voice behind him.

"Oh, I'm sorry. Didn't mean to startle you," said his second in command, walking into the laboratory.

Eric was relieved it was her and not someone else. "You've got cat's paws, Jane," he said.

Jane smiled. "And you've got the look of someone who just got caught doing something he's not supposed to be doing."

Eric raised his hands. "You got me. I was working on a Sunday."

"I can see that." Jane stopped by his side and looked at the computer screen. "Same weapon?"

"Apparently so." He tried to keep his tone of voice neutral, to hide how agitated he felt.

His colleague sighed. "I just stopped by to bring back my kit. I forgot it in the car, but something tells me I should stay a little while." She put her bag down on a chair nearby and ran her fingers through her hair.

"You should go," he said. "You, at least, have a life outside this office." Irony seemed like the best path to follow. Right now he needed to think things through carefully, and the last thing he wanted was Jane hanging around with him.

"Are you kidding?" she said, adjusting her ponytail. "We've got three homicides on our hands. Technically we can start talking about a serial killer. And two of those within the last couple of days to boot. For all we know, our killer might be out there right now, hunting down his next victim. We don't have any leads, and you expect me to wander on home? You should be calling everybody in here to work overtime!"

The new reality, the one that Eric knew and Jane did not, was that they had a lead—a big one—but in order to follow it Eric really needed to be alone.

Jane picked up her bag again. "I'm going to leave my stuff in my office. I'll be right back."

Just then the phone rang, and before Shaw could do anything, Jane answered and hit the speaker button.

"Ballistics lab, Jane Hall speaking."

"Oh . . . Detective Hall," said Mills hesitantly. "I was looking for Detective Shaw. We talked a little while ago." At this, Jane shot Eric an inquisitive glance.

"I'm here," said Eric, ignoring his colleague.

"Sorry for earlier. We got cut off, and I had to wait a little while before I called back because I think I saw some movement."

Jane's expression was eloquent: What?!

"Movement?" asked Eric. He didn't know what the officer was talking about either.

"As I was telling you, I looked into that thing you asked about, and you were right. It appears Ridley does have a connection with Christopher Garnish."

Hall's inquisitive expression turned into a look of confusion and preoccupation.

"The New Arts Gallery. I'm standing outside right now. The victim worked here, and as it turns out Garnish owns the place. And that's not all! Tom Ridley was Garnish's uncle on his mother's side."

This was news Eric wasn't expecting. The connection with the first two victims was weak—they'd done a little work together a number of years ago—but now there was an actual family relative involved. Every detail of the way they were killed was leading back to the 1994 case. Was it possible that all four were involved?

"Just a minute," said the detective, interrupting the flow of his thoughts. "You're outside the gallery right now?"

"Yes. I thought I'd come down and take a look around, even though I wasn't hoping for much, seeing as it's Sunday. But in the end I was lucky."

"Mills, don't do anything yet. Garnish might be extremely dangerous."

"No, of course not."

"You said you were lucky?" asked Jane.

"Yes, because the gallery is open on Sundays. I was just about to leave, but then I saw a woman unlock the place and go in. A little while later a man showed up too . . . For a moment I was hoping he was Garnish, but then I realized he's Muslim."

Eric wanted to drop everything he was doing, race down to meet Mills, and interrogate those two people, but that sort of impulsive and unexpected gesture would undoubtedly pique Jane's curiosity. He swore softly to himself but kept his outward calm.

"If you want . . . ," continued the officer, "I could go in and pretend to look at a few paintings."

"Do you have any idea who the woman is?"

"Well, given what I've seen so far, she might be Lorna Dillon. She works at the gallery too, and according to the people I spoke with, she might be Garnish's woman."

"Oh my God, Mills," interrupted Jane. "If that man is really involved in all these murders, I don't think it's a good idea for you to go around asking about his woman, at least not alone!"

"I agree," said Eric. "And in any case, I don't think Dillon would tell you where you can find him. Maybe you could continue to keep an eye on the place for a while, see what happens down there." He hoped he'd get a chance to free himself and go join the officer in the meantime. "If you see anything interesting, call me right away."

"Okay. We'll talk later."

Shaw hung up the phone.

"Why did he go down there alone?" Jane was nervous. Something didn't add up.

Eric decided to play the whole thing down. "Oh, you know how zealous Mills can be. Evidently he didn't have anything better to do today." He picked back up the bullet he'd been examining, tucked it into its envelope, and sealed the top.

"In fact, why isn't Miriam dealing with this stuff? She should be there with Mills," Eric added, waving his arm vaguely to his right.

FROM MINA'S BLOG

Lorna Dillon left the house early this morning—a strange act that took me by surprise. What did she have to do at that hour on a Sunday morning? I'd been keeping an eye on her for a while now, at least whenever I had a chance.

But now that I've finished the job with the other three, Garnish is all I've got left to do.

I know that I should have been more patient. Over the past few months I've only been able to see him a few times, even figuring out where he lives, but he never stayed in one place for very long.

I'd lost him again around a week earlier, but I wasn't worried. One way or another, Lorna would lead me to him. I was certain that Christopher was nervous about the deaths of his ex-accomplices. Who knew how he'd reacted to Ridley's death? Maybe he'd become a little less careful than before.

I followed Lorna all the way to the New Arts Gallery, going into the café across the street for a coffee. Sitting by the window, I pretended to be focused on my computer, when in reality I was keeping a close watch on the gallery. With the help of a little video camera hooked up to my PC, I was able to enlarge the image of the gallery and the exhibition room behind the window. Every once in a while a woman appeared in the frame, walking back and forth as if she were waiting for something.

I sat there awhile before I saw a man go in and talk to her briefly. Then he left. Lorna disappeared deeper into the gallery again and didn't reappear for at least a couple of hours. When she finally reappeared, she was holding her jacket and purse. She left and locked the door behind her, walking down the street.

I picked my stuff up right away and started following her.

It was pretty warm outside today. Evidently summer has arrived. I walked along with a map of the city in one hand and a camera in the other, blending in to look like a tourist. I kept my hair up beneath my baseball cap and wore a pair of dark sunglasses.

While I was walking, I pretended to follow a route on the map. Roughly twenty minutes later I found myself crossing Admiralty Arch and heading down the Mall toward Buckingham Palace. There were crowds all around me, people walking up and down along the tree-lined street on their way to or from the royal palace for the famous changing of the guards.

I had to speed up the pace. If I lost sight of her, I'd never find her again in those crowds. I could sense that she'd come here for a precise reason, and it certainly didn't have anything to do with tourism.

Near the Victoria Memorial, the crowds turned into an ordered mass lined behind the barriers set up for the ceremony. Police officers were standing around directing human traffic, preventing people from stopping for too long outside the palace gates.

Lorna stopped near the monument at the center of the roundabout. She looked around impatiently. I was roughly a dozen yards away from her, blending in with a group of Spanish boys, my eyes focused on her at every moment.

Then I saw him.

It was the first time I'd had a chance to see him clearly in the light of day. He wasn't much different from the man who had stood in my living room twenty years ago. He wasn't a young man anymore, but wasn't old like the other three either. I guessed he was a little over forty now. He was well dressed in a suit and tie, looking like any other businessman.

He came up to Lorna from behind, and as soon as she recognized him she gave him a giant hug. They seemed like a normal couple out for a Sunday-morning stroll, aside from the fact that, judging from their expressions, they weren't particularly happy at all. After the hug, the woman seemed upset and kept talking and making violent, brusque hand gestures. He listened to her without saying anything, keeping his eyes focused ahead and rarely turning to look at her. At a certain point his mouth moved and he said something. She nodded. Then Christopher turned around and started walking on alone in my direction.

I was forced to backpedal and hide in the crowd. He passed by me, barely two yards away, before crossing the street, then went into Green Park. I wanted to follow him, but the park was a lot less crowded, and I was afraid he might notice me. So I continued along the sidewalk running up Constitution Hill, keeping an eye on him from a distance while he walked along a park path. If he'd decided to cut through the park, I would've had to go in and follow him, hoping he wouldn't notice me. But I was lucky. When he reached the end of the park, he went back out on the road and headed for the entrance to the Hyde Park Corner tube station.

I went down the stairs, keeping my distance but careful not to lose track of him in that maze of underground corridors. I tried to walk close to other people so that I wouldn't look like I was alone.

When he reached the platform to take the northbound train, I stood at the opposite end. When the train came into the station, I waited until he'd gotten on board before doing the same, entering through the door at the far end of his car.

As I was getting aboard, a man passed by me in a rush, squeezing in and standing right in front of me. I had to lean to one side so that I could see Garnish's back. I didn't know where he was going, and I had to be careful if I wanted to see where he got off.

We crossed most of the city. People got on and off, except for the man standing in front of me, who was now the perfect shield. And except for me.

Finally we reached Arsenal station. Garnish moved to the door just as the train was slowing down. In that same moment, my shield turned and got ready to get off too. That's the first time I was able to see the shield's face: Mills. He didn't notice me at all, too busy watching elsewhere.

When Mills got off the train and started trailing Garnish, I realized he wasn't there by chance. For a moment I felt panic take over. If the police got to him now, it was all over. It was too early. I had to make sure that didn't happen.

I sped up so that I was just behind the policeman, who was pushing past people in a way that was anything but discreet. What an idiot. Garnish would see him.

People were slowing down at the staircase that led up to the street. A group of elderly ladies were walking slowly up the steps. I took advantage of them in order to move past Mills. Then I slipped in close to one of the ladies and gave her a little shove, just enough to make her lose her balance. The policeman grabbed her out of instinct, and a little crowd formed around them almost immediately. I barely maneuvered out, then threaded my way up the stairs in a hurry. All this happened behind Garnish, so he hadn't seen a thing and was continuing on his way. I stayed behind him, this time alone.

The neighborhood was practically deserted. I was afraid he might turn around and see me at any moment, so I decided to crouch behind cars as I followed. When he turned onto a street lined with houses, I waited at the corner. It was a long street with very few cross streets. He must be close to his destination, I thought. And in fact, a little while later he opened a little gate and walked up to a red and white house with a small courtyard out front. He opened the door with a key and disappeared inside.

Carefully I moved closer, keeping an eye on the windows. There was plenty of sunlight, and he would be able to see me from inside the house. A blue car was parked outside. It was his—I was sure of it. I'd already seen it several times before during the previous months. It was the only thing aside from his various commercial activities that was actually held in his name. The license plate checked out.

I wanted to wait until he left to go into the house, but who knew? Maybe he was about to abandon it altogether.

There was only one logical thing to do.

I moved to the car from the sidewalk, hiding behind it. I crouched down, removed my backpack, and took out a slim jim.

A guy like Garnish doesn't bother with alarms. He knows they're perfectly useless. If someone wants to steal a car, they'll do it, alarms or not. But then Garnish's car—an old, rundown Volkswagen—wasn't particularly attractive to thieves. It was part of his tendency to keep a low profile at all times.

It was easy to break the lock. I placed the slim jim back in the bag and put on a pair of latex gloves. I opened the door just enough to sneak in, slithering my way inside on the driver's side. Even though the car was old, the interior seemed new. The dashboard was clean, and there was no trash or clutter lying on the floor. Staying low, I reached up to the glove compartment. What I found when I opened it proved a pleasant surprise.

I'd guessed that he might keep a weapon in the car, but the fact that he had that particular model of nine-millimeter was a wonderful and lucky surprise. At first I'd thought I would have to hide my weapon underneath a car seat and hope he wouldn't notice it, but my discovery permitted me to use a different approach.

I took my pistol out of my backpack and exchanged it for the one he had in his glove compartment. He'd never realize the difference.

After taking a quick peek outside, I moved into the backseat. I lowered the seats so that I could get into the trunk, where I left another little present.

I indulged my own sense of triumph for a few moments. I knew I was close to completing my vendetta and that afterward I would finally be free.

What would I do then? I would no longer have a specific objective for my actions. Maybe I'd feel lost. I grew up in hatred, and I'm not sure I can live without it.

But no, I don't want to think about that right now.

When I raised my head a little, I noticed a man a bit off, standing still behind the car. I dropped back down instantly, my heart racing out of control. He was moving slowly along the sidewalk. I couldn't see who it was, but in any case I could no longer slip out of the car and walk away.

There was the sound of an engine outside, then the squeal of brakes. A car pulled backward in reverse and came to a stop right alongside Garnish's vehicle. The man on the sidewalk crossed the narrow street and went over to the car that had just pulled up. I heard voices. Mills. He was talking with the driver. I couldn't understand what they were saying.

I took a chance and raised my head up so that I could see the other person. Eric! He was driving the car!

Suddenly I found it hard to breathe. Garnish might walk out that door any minute now, or the two outside Garnish's car might realize I was here. Or worse yet, both things might happen! Everything would be over just like that.

But for some reason, the intense fear I felt also made me incredibly excited. In that moment, I felt more alive than I'd ever felt in my life. For several years now, danger had been like a drug for me. For a fraction of a second I even contemplated getting out of the car as if it were nothing and simply walking away. I knew I could do it. It seemed like a wonderful idea, really.

Then Mills walked around Eric's car and got into the passenger seat, and the car drove away.

I watched them as they took off. I was almost disappointed, like a little girl after her favorite doll gets taken away. Then I gathered up my things, took one last look at the house, got out of the car, then walked away in the direction from which I'd come.

CHAPTER 13

The apartment had been searched from top to bottom. Things were lying here and there. The drawers had been emptied. The shattered pieces of a few porcelain knickknacks knocked off one of the shelves, now tilted into a table, lay scattered across the floor. A man's legs stuck out from underneath the table.

Dr. Dawson waited for his turn while two agents tried to lift up the shelf without disturbing anything else.

"Easy, easy!" urged Miriam, raising her hand to wave to Eric.

"Good morning, Detective," said the doctor. "We seem to be starting our days off like this a little too often lately."

"Morning," said Shaw, laconic.

"On three . . ." The agents almost had it. "One, two, and . . . three!"

The shelf came up, but a picture frame slipped off and came crashing down on the body.

Dawson released a deep, sonorous sigh. "Eyes on the prize, gentlemen!"

Jane walked in from the other room. "Ah, you got it." A big camera was hanging from a strap around her neck. She had to practically climb over the doctor in order to get closer to the body, since Dawson was now crouching down by the victim, pulling on a pair of latex gloves. That's when Jane finally noticed Eric. "Hey there . . . Sorry, I didn't see you," she said, smiling at her boss.

"You alone?" asked the detective. Usually another member of the team would be present.

"For the moment, yes. I talked to Adele a little while ago. She was stuck in traffic but on her way. I sent her the exact address via cell."

"What do we know?" Eric scrutinized the confusion surrounding them. "Seems like there was a struggle."

"Two bullet wounds, one in the chest and another in the head," said Dawson, who had begun examining the body.

"I take that back," Dawson added quickly.

The doctor was taking a closer look at the victim's hands. "No signs he defended himself, but . . ." He paused at the wrists. "I see signs he was tied up." Dawson turned to look at the two criminologists. "I'm betting he was tied up and then killed later. Maybe the assassin was looking for something." His eyes moved around to take in the entire room.

"Not just here," said Jane, stooping to photograph the victim's wrists. "The same hurricane swept through the other rooms too."

"The assassin must have found what he was looking for; after that he no longer needed this guy," said Eric. Maybe the crime was drug-related. More often than not, that's what it all came down to.

"So . . . ," said Detective Leroux, pausing. She had finished talking with the other agents. "The apartment belongs to a certain . . ." She stopped and reread notes she'd taken on her smartphone. "Daniel Pennington."

Eric froze the moment he heard that last name. "Come again?"

"Did you say Pennington?" asked Jane.

Shaw went over to the body and knelt down beside it. The face was turned to one side, a lock of hair covering the mouth. He moved it. "Oh fuck."

There was a rustle of noise outside the room. Someone was coming in a hurry.

"Danny!"

Eric leapt to his feet. "No, no!" He ran to the door.

He made it just in time to intercept Adele and keep her from coming in.

"Danny! No!" she cried. "No!"

The detective held on to her, but Adele was hysterical, and her anguish gave her incredible strength. "Why?" she shouted, waving her arms, struggling to break away from him.

"Calm down. You have to calm down!" said Eric, his tone emotional but firm. "It's better if you don't go in."

Adele didn't even seem to hear him. "No! What have they done . . . Danny?" Her face was livid, all the muscles jumping and contracting.

Detective Hall went over to them, blocking the corpse from view. "Sweetheart, please . . . Please calm down." She spoke in a maternal voice, caressing Adele's head while Eric fought to hold her.

He was afraid he might hurt her, but he didn't know what else he could do to help. Seeing her like this broke his heart.

Eventually Adele stopped struggling and began to weep, sliding down until she was on her knees, dragging Eric along with her. She began hiccupping so forcefully that her entire body shook.

"They have the same last name," muttered Miriam, who'd come up behind Hall. "Who was he? Her brother?"

"Her ex-husband," said Eric.

"I'll handle this," said Jane, pushing Miriam away. "I'll call someone else from the lab. Take her outside."

Eric picked Adele up, and she stopped crying almost instantly. She looked up at him, an expression of utter stupor on her face. Suddenly she went rigid. Her eyes rolled up into her head, her hands balled into fists, and her body began to shake with powerful spasms.

"Richard!" shouted Shaw, putting her back down on the floor. "She's having convulsions!"

The doctor ran to him. "Turn her head to one side," he said, already reaching to do so with both hands. "Make sure she can breathe freely. Looks like an epileptic fit."

"I didn't know she suffered from epilepsy," said Jane, who had knelt by Adele's side and was caressing her arm. "She's always so reserved. How did you know she was married?" Then she made a quick expression of disgust, realizing what a dumb question it was.

All she got by way of answer was a severe glare from her boss. This was hardly the moment for that conversation, even though Eric knew full well that Hall would approve of any kind of relationship between him and Pennington.

"I called for an ambulance," said Miriam, sticking her head back in through the doorway. "They'll be here shortly."

Someone shook him, and he opened his eyes. For a moment he was disoriented. He couldn't remember where he was. Then he felt someone touch his shoulder, and he turned around.

"Sorry," whispered Jane. "I didn't realize you were sleeping."

The hospital room was in shadows, and Eric had fallen asleep in the armchair set alongside Adele's bed.

"I didn't get enough sleep last night," he said, massaging his neck with one hand. He'd unbuttoned the top of his oxford and loosened his tie. As soon as he moved, the jacket lying over the arm of the chair slipped onto the floor.

Jane collected it and sat down in a chair across from him. "How is she doing?"

"They gave her a sedative. She's been asleep for hours. The doctor said she had a violent attack." He yawned and grimaced. "What time is it?"

"Around three in the afternoon. Have you had anything to eat?"

Who could be hungry at a time like this? "How did things go at the crime scene?"

"That's why I'm here," said Jane. She hung the jacket over the back of her chair and leaned toward him. She looked worried. "As soon as we brought the body to the morgue, Richard extracted the bullet from the man's chest. It will take him longer to recover the other one."

Eric could tell from her tone of voice that bad news was on the way.

"As soon as I saw it was a nine-millimeter, I decided to compare it to the others."

No. Again?

Jane nodded in response to her colleague's worried eyes. "The same weapon," she said.

"The same weapon?" Adele's voice made them both turn around.

"Hey . . . ," murmured Eric, extending his hand to hers. "How are you feeling?" His mind was a storm of contrasting emotions.

Adele's face was dark, devoid of light. She looked absolutely exhausted. "Danny is dead."

"I'm sorry . . ."

"He killed him too . . ." It wasn't a question; it was an observation.

Shaw didn't know what to say. He turned and looked at Jane for help, but for once not even she could come up with anything comforting to say. Discovering a connection between this homicide and the other murders seemed to knock them back to ground zero, dismantling all the theories they'd come up with over the past few days. Why would Garnish kill Daniel Pennington? It's true they didn't know much about the victim, but the way he was murdered was completely different from the meticulous modus operandi the killer had employed in the other killings. The only connection was the pistol.

He wiped his hand across his forehead. His head was pounding and fit to explode with the effort he was making to try to ferret some sense out of all this. It didn't make any sense at all. The key had to be

Garnish—he was sure of it. Maybe Garnish had realized he was being followed by Mills and had seen them when Eric went to pick up the officer near Arsenal stadium. Maybe that drove him to change his plans.

He looked at Adele. She seemed lost in her own thoughts. He wanted to ask her a million questions about her ex-husband, to try and figure out what kind of connection there might be, but this was anything but the right moment . . .

"I'll leave you two alone," said Jane, getting up.

Eric had completely forgotten she was there. "Oh, that's not necessary . . . ," he said, but it was a timid protest.

"I have to get back to the department." She put her hand on his arm. "You go ahead and stay here. I'll take care of everything. We'll see each other tomorrow." She turned to Adele but didn't say anything. Adele had closed her eyes again.

As soon as the door closed, Adele stirred and squeezed Eric's hand.

"You really scared us," said Eric, smiling at her.

The corners of her mouth turned up for a moment. "I haven't had an attack in a long time," she said. When she mentioned her epilepsy, her eyes stared out at nothing, focusing on a point somewhere in the distance.

"It's been a really bad day," Eric added limply.

"Yeah." Adele seemed to come back and focus on him again. "We grew up together. Did I ever tell you that? Danny and I." She took a long, deep breath, turning her head to the window. A faint light came in through the drawn blinds. They could hear rain outside, pattering on the windowpane. "He was my first best friend. The first boy I ever kissed. The first boy I . . . was ever with." She laughed a little to herself. "It was a disaster."

Eric couldn't help but chuckle along with her.

"I should have seen back then that I *really* wasn't his type."

It was nice to see her smile again, even if only to remember someone who had passed.

"But I still agreed to marry him, because he loved me, in his own way. And I loved him. What's the term for that, the one Americans use to call a woman like me?"

Eric looked at her, perplexed. How was he supposed to know?

"A fag hag!" she said, laughing. "God I loved his friends. We were a great group."

"You were married while he spent time with other gay men?" he asked. She never stopped surprising him. Or maybe he was just too old for this kind of thing.

"Oh sure. They thought I was his sister because of the last name. They never imagined that I was his wife!"

She'd married her gay best friend and taken his last name so that she could pretend to be his sister. It was amazing how little he really knew about this woman. But once again, he felt like all these new and surprising tidbits did nothing but increase how attractive she was to him.

"You guys lived together, but dated other people?"

"Of course! Then we shared all the details."

"But why did you even get married in the first place?"

Adele shrugged. "Something to do." Then, suddenly, she turned serious. "I considered him my family. Marrying him, I thought he really would be." She sighed. "I know. It doesn't make any sense."

"There is a certain logic to it," admitted Eric. "Though it's not something you see every day."

"You can say that again."

"Why did you two get divorced?"

"We realized that being married didn't make sense anymore. Back then he'd started a serious relationship, at least that's what he said, but I kept living with him for a few years while we waited for the divorce to become final—just like the sister everybody thought I was. Then I started to feel a need for a space all my own."

"But you kept his last name."

"I told you, he's like a brother to me. More than a brother." Suddenly her face darkened. "*Was* like a brother."

"Then what happened?" Eric asked immediately, trying to draw her attention away from darker thoughts and lead her to happier ones.

"Well, he and his boyfriend broke up, just as I'd imagined they would." She laughed.

"What about you?"

"Me? Nothing. I didn't want to get involved in a serious relationship." She drew a finger across her lips. "Of course I didn't exactly lock myself up in a convent, if that's what you mean."

Eric felt himself flare up and immediately tried to calm himself down again.

"I had my *adventures*, but nothing important. Nobody was good enough."

"Because nobody was like him," added Shaw.

Adele nodded, then squeezed his hand again. "Or like you," she said, shooting him a mischievous glance.

Eric preferred not to try to explain Adele's behavior. That simple glance was enough to make him feel good inside. During the hours she'd been asleep he had racked his brain with questions, wondering whether or not she would be happy to see him there once she woke up. The fact that she was playing with him again didn't seem all that important right now. After everything that had happened to her, he felt willing to forgive her just about anything, even something incomprehensible. Part of him, however, still held out hope that she was being sincere.

"When can I get up and get out of here?" said Adele, interrupting his thoughts.

"Right away, I think. As long as you feel up to it. They were waiting for you to wake up again before discharging you."

"I want to go home."

"I don't think you should be alone right now."

Adele let go of his hand. "I'm used to it," she said, drawing her arm tight across her chest.

"I'm serious."

She scrutinized him.

"You've had a rough time," he continued. "You have to let someone help take care of you, at least for a few days."

She groaned a little. "I don't have anyone to ask."

"You have me." He'd finally summoned his courage and said it. He could feel the adrenaline coursing through his body.

Adele seemed surprised. "Nice move, Detective!" Then she laughed a little. "Thank God I asked you to take it slow for a while."

Okay, he expected that. He knew she'd probably insist on misinterpreting his gesture. Eric himself wondered if he didn't have ulterior motives, but it was true that she needed to be taken care of. He laughed too. "I'm not trying to seduce you," he said, raising both hands. "I swear! I'm just worried about you."

She smiled. Maybe she was considering his offer.

Outside, he opened the door to the black SUV like a true gentleman, which seemed to make an impression on her. Or at least that was the reaction Adele chose to reveal.

The rain had stopped. A wash of blue crossed the sky, ending in a glimmer of freshly revealed sunlight that brightened the entire Monday.

The doctor had discharged her in the late afternoon, and in the end she gave in to Eric, but insisted it would not be for more than a couple of days. "So you *do* have a car!" she exclaimed, climbing into the passenger seat.

Eric closed the door behind her, then walked around the car and got into the driver's seat. Glancing at her, he could see that she was staring at him, waiting for an answer. "Well, yeah," he said. "I have a car. And as I'm sure you can see, it's not exactly the best vehicle in the world for moving around a crowded city." Not to mention the fact that it took him far less time to get to Scotland Yard in the tube, even though he had his own reserved parking space in the department lot. Whenever he drove anywhere else, however, he couldn't count on such a privilege.

"I hope you take it out and use it every once in a while. It would be a shame to leave a beauty like this rotting away in the garage."

Eric turned the key, making the engine roar and getting Adele to laugh. "Oh, I use it all right."

"When? You're always working!"

They slowly pulled out of the hospital parking lot, then got on a minor highway.

"Whenever I can, I get away and go to my country cottage. It's one of the few things my ex left me."

"A country cottage . . ." Adele lingered over those words. "Sounds romantic," she added, giving him a sensual wink.

"Remarkably romantic," said Eric. He was struggling to keep his eyes on the road.

That morning she had discovered that her ex-husband was dead, and now here she was flirting with Eric. It was hard to say just how reliable Adele was. She seemed to change moods and ideas from one moment to the next, forcing Shaw to keep on his toes.

They crossed through the city without saying much else, making it all the way to Dorset Street in silence. Eric pulled over near the entrance to Adele's apartment building.

"I'm going to go up and grab a few things," she said, about to open the door. But then she stopped. "Just a minute. My car is still parked at the crime scene. My kit is inside too." Then she looked around, alarmed. "Where's my gun? I had it with me!"

"Don't worry. Your kit and pistol are in the trunk." He jerked his thumb toward the back. "I had someone bring that beater you're driving here." He took her keys out of his pocket and used them to point ahead. A red Ford sat parked at the end of the road. Just then he remembered that she'd said it belonged to her sister-in-law. "Hold on, the sister-in-law you talked about, the owner of that car . . . is she Daniel's sister?"

Adele shook her head. "She's the sister of Daniel's ex-boyfriend. Seeing as how everybody thought I was his sister . . ." She didn't finish the sentence because her meaning was clear. "I should call her, tell her what's happened."

"You can take care of that later."

She nodded, taking her keys from his hand and getting out of the SUV.

Eric watched her walk away until she'd entered her building, then sighed and relaxed in his seat. His eyes wandered around, passing across the rearview mirror. A dark car had pulled in and parked right behind his. The driver was still in the car and appeared to have no intention of getting out.

He turned around to take a better look. Even though the man was wearing a pair of dark sunglasses that prevented Eric from seeing his eyes, Shaw had the distinct impression he was being watched.

A moment later the engine turned over and the car moved. When it passed his SUV, Eric saw that the car was an old, dark-blue Volkswagen. He had the feeling he'd seen it before, but he couldn't remember where.

Twenty minutes after she'd gone in, Adele reappeared outside the building. She opened the rear door and tossed in a big black bag, then climbed into the front passenger seat. "Did it," she said, pulling on her seat belt.

Still thoughtful, Eric turned his car on.

"You can set yourself up in here." Eric put Adele's bag on the queen-sized bed while she watched, perplexed, from the doorway. She was still holding her kit and gun.

"Don't worry," said Eric. "I'm sleeping in Brian's room."

The woman frowned and walked into the room, suspicious.

"Brian's my son. Sometimes he comes over to spend the weekend here with me."

"Ah, right. Your son." Now she seemed to relax a little. She put her things down on the nightstand and turned her attention to the big bag, digging out her laptop.

"I'll make some room for you in the closet," said Eric, moving things around.

Adele put the computer down on the little table by the window and moved the bag onto the floor. Then she took off her shoes and stretched out on the bed to relax. Eric turned around every once in a while to look at her.

She was so beautiful. He had to summon all his strength to keep from being overtly distracted. He emptied two drawers and moved his clothing to one side of the closet. Now there was a little more room.

When he turned around again, he found her staring back at him, her head tilted to one side and an astute smile on her face. She was incredibly seductive. He told himself she must still be in shock, and that's why she was behaving so strangely. She wasn't trying to provoke him, even though it sure seemed like she was.

"Okay," said Eric, satisfied with himself. "Now you can put your stuff away."

"You're a really handsome man, do you know that?"

Adele's comment left Eric speechless for a moment. "Thanks," he managed finally, finding nothing better to say. "You're not bad yourself."

She laughed. "I know you'd like to jump all over me right now."

Was it that obvious? No, nonsense. She was doing it on purpose just to needle him. She had a very peculiar way of dealing with bereavement.

"Is it just me, or weren't you the one who said we have to take things slow?"

"You didn't exactly agree, if I remember correctly." Adele's expression changed to vague boredom. She got up and went over to the bathroom, but didn't go in. She simply stood in the doorway and looked around. She seemed like someone visiting a museum.

Eric felt all his self-imposed restraint come crashing down around him in an instant. Gripped by an unexpected resoluteness, he walked quickly across the room to her, taking Adele by the shoulders and spinning her around. "You have to stop playing with me, little lady."

She stared up at him, startled. There seemed to be a tenuous light of possibility deep in her eyes.

But before Adele could say anything, Eric grabbed her and kissed her. He didn't stop, not even when Adele seemed indifferent, unwilling to kiss him back. But she didn't stay that way for long.

Suddenly they were both fighting off their clothing, struggling to be free.

He hadn't felt this good in a long, long time. He couldn't even remember the last time. It all felt impossible, hard to believe it was real. But there she was, stretched out alongside him, her face still flushed, her expression relaxed and her beautiful hair splayed out across the pillows. She stared into his eyes, her finger tracing an imaginary path through his hair, then down his neck and across his chest. She had a little tattoo of a lotus flower on one wrist. Who knew what story lay behind that small symbol?

"You're a surprising man."

"Handsome and surprising. You're all compliments today," said Eric. He took her hand and brought it to his mouth for a kiss.

Adele threw her head back and laughed.

Eric turned toward her, and the two stared into one another's eyes for a while. "Should I feel guilty I've just slept with a *girl*?" he asked in a joking tone, then tilted his head and rolled his eyes back and forth, pretending to consider the question honestly. Finally he shook his head violently. "No, not even a little bit."

"I'm a woman, not a girl," she protested, but she smiled as she said it and gave him a light punch in the shoulder.

"Definitely not," said Eric, his eyes opening wide in pretend shock. "Girls don't know how to do certain things."

Adele laughed again.

"But maybe," continued Eric in the same playful tone of voice as before, "I should feel guilty because I'm also your boss?" Then he shook his head again. "Definitely not!"

"Hmm . . . Maybe I should sue you for sexual harassment."

"You'd better not," he said, reaching out for her body and tickling her sides.

"No, no, please! No torture! I'll confess to anything you want. It's all my fault!" Then she dissolved into giggling.

Suddenly a ray of sunlight broke through the clouds, shone through the window, and filled the room with golden light. It was so beautiful and surprising that the couple stopped fooling around and turned to look out the window. Dancing ribbons of light played across the bedsheets.

"It stopped raining," said Eric. He'd lost all sense of time. He hadn't taken a day off in at least a year, and he wasn't used to being home during the day in the middle of a workweek, even in the late afternoon—much less in the company of a woman.

He got up to move the curtains and let as much sunlight in as possible. Standing next to the window, he turned to look at Adele, who had sat up in bed. Her naked body practically sparkled in the sunlight. She was truly, incredibly beautiful. For a moment he was almost afraid of his depth of feeling for her. Everything had happened so quickly. He wasn't sure he deserved all this, deserved her.

In order to hide the emotions he was feeling, Eric turned back around and stared out the window. There was the usual to-and-fro of pedestrians. Two kids were running along the sidewalk on the other side of the street. A woman was following them, shouting, and the two children stopped, but only because a boy with a big dog on a leash was bearing down on them from the other direction. Eric smiled. He remembered when Brian was little and how hard it was for him and Crystal to rein in their son's exuberance.

Then, by chance, his eye was drawn farther down the street, to the right. A blue car was parked along the side of the road. He recognized it immediately. It was identical to the Volkswagen he'd seen near Adele's house.

"What's up?" asked Adele, sensing something was wrong. He heard her get up and come over to the window. She looked out in the same direction.

"That car," said Eric. "The blue one. I saw one that looked just like it outside your house. When the driver realized I was looking at him, he turned the car on and drove away."

She squinted at the car. "There's somebody inside."

The car was in shadow, and it wasn't easy to see anything more.

"I don't like it," said Eric, turning to look for his phone.

"Wait," said Adele, going over to her purse and taking out her smartphone. She went back to the window, then used the phone to zoom in on the car's license plate and take a picture. "There. It's pretty clear."

"Send it to Stern." Shaw took his cordless phone off the nightstand and called the desk where the criminologist usually sat.

"Hey, boss," said Stern, displaying an easiness he didn't actually possess.

"Stern, Adele's about to send you a license plate number. Check it out and let me know who it belongs to, okay?"

"Okay, yes," said Stern, his voice pitched too high with excitement. "Got the message. I'll check right away."

Eric hit the speakerphone button and put the cordless down on the bed. Adele was getting dressed, and he did too, keeping his eye on the car outside the window. It was still there, its driver still sitting patiently.

"Boss," said the voice on the telephone. He seemed agitated. "The owner is Christopher Garnish, the guy we're looking for!"

"Fuck!" exclaimed Eric, pulling on his shoes. "Send backup to my house immediately."

"Immediately . . . to your house?" said the criminologist, but then Eric hung up, cutting him off.

"What do you want to do?" asked Adele.

Eric grabbed his holster and gun and put them on. Then he took another look out the window. "Arrest him," he said.

Adele grabbed his arm, her mouth open in surprise. "Aren't you going to wait for the backup?"

But Eric broke free from her grip and headed for the door.

"Wait!" she said, grabbing her own gun off the floor. "I'm coming with you!"

Together they left the apartment and went down into the lobby.

Shaw held the building door open just a crack to take a look around outside. The Volkswagen was still there. The man behind the wheel seemed to be watching a couple who was walking past on the sidewalk. When the driver turned his head toward the passenger seat, tracking the couple, Eric and Adele went outside and moved down the street. They held their guns hidden behind their backs and approached the car from behind so they wouldn't be noticed.

The man in the blue car raised his head, his face turning to the rear-view mirror. He was still wearing dark sunglasses, so it was impossible to see where he was focusing his gaze, but he had undoubtedly noticed them. The way he tensed and froze gave him away.

The detectives moved quickly, but the man started his car immediately. Eric ran to get in front of the car and block him from leaving. "Stop! Police!" But instead of stopping, the driver accelerated.

"Watch out!" cried Adele.

Shaw jumped out of the way just in time, barely avoiding being hit by the car.

"Son of a bitch!" Eric stared at the car racing away. He raised his arm toward the car, ready to shoot at it, but then stopped himself. It was already too far away. "Fuck . . . ," he murmured to himself. He put his hand in his pocket and pulled out a set of keys.

"Let's take my car," he said to Adele, pointing to the SUV.

They jumped in and started after the blue car, turning on the siren and emergency lights installed on the dashboard.

"You may not use this car very much, but you've got it pretty well equipped!" said Adele, struggling to latch her seat belt while Eric accelerated and swerved around other vehicles.

The Volkswagen turned left on Gloucester Place, racing at high speed and cutting off another car coming from the right. A cacophony of angry honking filled the air just as Eric came racing in behind him and did the same thing.

The streetlight up ahead was green, but it turned yellow just as Garnish was crossing Marylebone, overtaking a van and heading toward Park Road. A moment later it turned red, but Eric didn't slow down. The sound of screeching brakes accompanied them as they shot through the intersection. A motorcyclist heading into the intersection swerved, lost control of the bike, and tumbled across the pavement. The detective saw him get up in his rearview mirror and give him the finger. Evidently he wasn't hurt too badly.

"We're nearly to the A41. If he keeps going this way, we'll lose him!" exclaimed Adele.

"Fuck! I know!" Eric accelerated, but the Volkswagen was much more agile in traffic than his hulking SUV. Sunlight streaming in from low on the horizon got in his eyes too, making his pursuit that much more difficult.

They reached a large roundabout and headed onto Wellington Road. Ahead of them, but not by much, the streetlight turned green. Garnish had plenty of open road and accelerated even faster. At that very moment a pedestrian stepped into the crosswalk. Garnish's car swerved just in time, smashing into a low sign on the traffic island. This slowed the car just enough for the light to turn yellow, but Garnish accelerated again.

At the next intersection, he was blocked by a bus, while the right lane was partially obstructed by a delivery truck pulling out to turn around. The bus slowed down to stop at the light.

"Gotcha!" said Eric, smiling to himself.

But Garnish wasn't going to give up that easily. He slammed on the brakes, pulled to a stop, and jumped out of the car. He left it there on the side of the road and took off running across the street.

Eric stopped behind the Volkswagen and jumped out, gun in hand, ready to chase after him.

"Eric!" cried Adele. Then came the sound of the door slamming and footsteps behind him.

Garnish seemed to be in excellent shape. He leapt and slid across the top of a car maneuvering to park, angering its driver, then headed down Circus Road. Running down the sidewalk, he slammed into two girls, knocking them both down.

"Police!" cried Eric. "Move aside! Stop right there!"

The suspect kept running. When he reached the second block, he turned right.

Shaw, who had just made it to the end of the first block, heard Adele's voice behind him, but when he turned around she was nowhere to be seen. He couldn't stop now.

He followed Garnish down a parallel street, which was much narrower than the one they'd been on and completely empty. The man had gained quite a few yards on him, and Eric could feel his lungs burning. His legs refused to move as quickly as he wanted them to.

He realized the street Garnish was on was a dead end. He was trapped. But Garnish dashed to the right, disappearing from view. Eric ran as quickly as he could, finally reaching a little pedestrian alley that ran between two buildings. Garnish had almost reached the far end. If he made it, he'd be out on a much larger, busier avenue.

Eric had lost him. He couldn't keep up.

Suddenly a small figure stepped out, blocking the end of the alley and aiming a gun directly at Garnish.

"Race is over," said Adele.

Garnish slipped and almost fell, trying to come to a stop. He started to raise his hands.

"Don't move!" shouted Eric, coming up behind him. Now that they were close, he could see that Garnish was somewhat shorter than he was. Probably around five foot nine, just like the black figure in their videos.

The suspect laughed humorlessly. "Hey, hey, hey . . . No need to point that thing at me," he said, keeping his eyes on Adele.

Shaw was patting him down, his sides, his legs. He was clean.

"I almost wish you would move," said Adele, her gun steady, pointed directly at Garnish.

The man laughed again. "I'm unarmed, and I haven't done anything. Unless I'm mistaken, it's not illegal to go running."

"It is if the police have ordered you to stop," said Eric, taking out his cell phone and bringing it to his ear.

"Terribly sorry. I must not have heard you."

He was playing with them, and neither one of them was enjoying it. After their mad dash through the streets of London, Shaw would gladly have punched his lights out, but a group of curious onlookers was gathering not far behind Adele.

"Stern," replied the officer at the other end at last.

"We've got Garnish. Send those reinforcements to the corner of Cochrane Street and . . ." He looked around. What the heck was the name of this alley?

"Cochrane Mews," said one of the bystanders. They could already hear sirens screaming in the distance.

CHAPTER 14

Miriam pounded both fists on the table in the interrogation room, playing yet another turn as bad cop. She stuck her face in close to Christopher Garnish.

"We know you killed those three people. You'd better come clean about it!"

"Oh yeah?" said Garnish, challenging her. "If you had any proof, I'd already be formally arrested, but that doesn't seem to be the case, does it?" He acted sure of himself, but a large bead of sweat was trickling down past his temple, betraying his true state of mind.

"It's just a matter of time," said Miriam calmly, throwing Eric a glance. Shaw was sitting facing the suspect, saying nothing.

Eric's hands were folded on the table, a file underneath them. Three photographs of the victims were spread across the tabletop. He kept the photo of the last victim close.

"At this very moment, officers are turning your apartment inside out, and I'm sure they'll find something," continued Detective Leroux.

"Don't be too sure, darling," said Garnish. He brought a hand up to his chin and cradled it. He seemed almost bored. Every once in a while he glanced at his wristwatch. Then a perplexed look came over his face. "My apartment?" he said. "How do you know where I live?"

"I think I've seen your car somewhere before," said Eric, speaking for the first time. That blue Volkswagen was really familiar. He'd seen an identical one just the day before when he'd gone to pick up Mills near Arsenal stadium. It hadn't been hard to describe the precise location to the officers. The owner of the house where the Volkswagen had been parked immediately recognized a photograph of the suspect.

There was a knock on the door; it opened and an officer stuck his head in. He motioned to Miriam.

"Excuse me a moment," she said, then left the room.

"So, Detective, how's life?" Garnish asked mockingly.

There was something in the man's voice, but Eric couldn't quite tell what it was.

"As long as we've got time to kill while we wait for my lawyer, we might as well have a nice little chat!" Then he laughed.

Shaw shook his head just a little, then opened the file. He took three photographs out and tossed them in front of Christopher.

Garnish froze, tense, but did nothing else.

"See any resemblance?" Shaw asked.

Garnish's face relaxed, his mouth widening into a smile. "You believe I should?" Now he was the one challenging Eric.

"This family was massacred in 1994." Eric pointed to the photographs he'd just tossed on the table. "Incredibly enough, each family member was killed in the exact same manner your friends were."

"Goodness gracious. Well. Looks like you're perfectly right, officer." He pretended to examine the photographs carefully, as if he were truly interested. "Except for the fact that these three losers, and I'm including my uncle in that list, weren't my friends."

"You and I both know it was you."

"Detective, Detective," said Christopher, taking him to task, "I'm perfectly familiar with your *alternative* methods, but I'm sure you're not so skilled that you can pin murders committed twenty years ago on me."

"But I *can* connect you to the ones committed over the past couple of weeks," Shaw said, staring Garnish dead in the eyes, though Christopher didn't seem particularly bothered by his words. "Including the murder committed last night," he added, tossing a photo of Daniel Pennington's body on the table in front of the suspect.

This time he got an immediate reaction. "What the hell's this supposed to mean?"

"All the murders were committed with the same weapon," said Eric, pointing to each photo in turn. "All I need to do is connect you to one of them, and then you're screwed."

Now Garnish seemed unsettled, agitated. "No." He shook his head. "It can't be." He took a deep breath and met Shaw's gaze. "I have an alibi," he added, resolute. "Last night I was with Lorna Dillon, my girlfriend. All night long. She can confirm that."

"What about the night between Friday and Saturday? What about the night between last Monday and Tuesday? How about June 12 around five thirty?" Eric shot questions rapid fire, one after the other, raising his voice a little with each one.

Garnish's mouth began to tremble just a little. "I was with her, every night . . ."

Yes, of course he was. Eric smiled. He could tell Garnish was cracking.

Suddenly the door swung open.

"We're done here," said a thirtysomething gentleman with an arrogant manner. He was dressed in an elegant, trendy suit and held a little leather briefcase in one hand. Unquestionably a lawyer. "I'm John Meyers, Mr. Garnish's lawyer."

What a surprise.

Christopher smiled at the sight of his savior.

"If you cannot place my client at the scene of the crime, then I'm afraid you have no further reason to keep him here," the suit said to Shaw.

He was right. Up until now they'd been biding time in order to give the other officers a chance to conduct searches, but in reality they didn't have the authority to keep Garnish in custody in the meantime. And without any proof, the crown prosecutor wouldn't even accuse Garnish. Other prosecutors had attempted to bring Garnish to justice in the past—tried and failed. The current prosecutor wasn't willing to waste time trying to bring him down again or make himself look ridiculous in the process.

"Therefore, Mr. Garnish and I are leaving. Right now. Come along, Christopher."

Garnish leapt to his feet and rushed to his lawyer's side. He was saved, but he still rubbed his fingers nervously across his stomach.

Eric was furious and doing everything he could not to smack this *insolent boy* in the face. He hated defense lawyers, especially those that hung around with shady characters like Garnish.

He looked at the two for a moment, then noticed Miriam standing out in the corridor behind them. She spread her arms and shrugged. She couldn't do anything about it.

The lawyer and his client disappeared into the hallway, followed by Detective Leroux.

At that point Eric lost control, knocking all the photos and paperwork off the table with an enraged sweep of his hand. They flew all over the room, fluttering against the two-way mirror and down onto the floor.

Turning around, he saw Adele standing at the door, staring at him with mild astonishment in her eyes.

Shaw grunted with disappointment. "Fuck!" he yelled. He closed his eyes and breathed deeply, leaning against the wall with one hand.

Adele walked over and embraced him.

That simple gesture slowly but surely calmed Eric down. He hugged her close and waited for his breathing to slow.

Adele lifted her head and looked up at him. "You'll see. It's not over yet."

"You can bet on it," he said. His frustration was dissipating. That was right, though. The bastard wouldn't get away with it. He ran a hand over his hair. "You're tired," he said to her.

"I'm okay," murmured Adele.

"No." He pulled the keys to his car out of his pocket and handed them to her. "Go home. You shouldn't even be here, not today. I'll meet you there later."

Adele was clearly reluctant, but she took the keys anyway. "Okay."

Officer Gordon opened the door to the blue Volkswagen and sat down in the passenger seat. Now what?

A tow truck had brought the car to the scientific investigations lab, and now he and Officer Smith were supposed to inspect it from end to end. A first scan hadn't revealed anything. The car seemed clean, including the glove compartment, which held nothing more than the vehicle documents and a few old CDs.

His colleague was going through the trunk, which was full of absurd items. Unlike the interior, which was practically immaculate, the trunk was stuffed with all sorts of things: work tools, snacks that seemed to have fossilized in their packaging, a rolled-up rug, paint cans and brushes, a bag full of jogging clothes. The bag, when opened, enveloped the criminologist with a foul wave of rotting sweat. The man, accustomed to handling much worse, coughed a little and fought back nausea.

Inside the car, in the meantime, Gordon was already resigned. He would have to take this thing apart piece by piece. He got out and pushed the seat he'd been sitting in all the way back, then took out his flashlight and knelt over to take a look underneath.

Nothing there.

He got up and walked around the car, doing the same with the other seats. Each time he walked around the rear end of the vehicle, he took a look at the things that Smith was pulling out of the trunk and checking, one by one.

Gordon opened a rear door and reached out for the lever that would bring the seats down. He found it and pulled, but the seats wouldn't budge, so he put his little flashlight in his mouth and grabbed the seat with both hands, yanking on it. No use; it was stuck.

"Fuck me," he muttered, crouching down and using his flashlight to try and see what silly little bit of nothing was stuck in the tracks, preventing the seat from moving.

And there it was.

"I can't believe it!" He reached out with one gloved hand and tried to touch the object, regretting he wasn't limber like his younger colleagues.

Finally he got ahold of it and pulled the object out. "Smith, I've got something," he said. His colleague stuck his head around the back of the car and found Gordon holding up something metallic with two fingers. The nine-millimeter.

"Fuck me too!" exclaimed Smith. "Look what I found hidden underneath the carpeting back here!" He was holding up one arm with a long black outfit draped over it, while his other hand held a small, dark metal cylinder. A silencer.

"I'll give you a hand."

Eric turned around as soon as he heard Jane's voice. She was holding a few pages of the file he'd tossed across the interrogation room.

The woman bent down to pick up the other pages, then stood up slowly, her eyes fixed on what she now held in her hands. "What's this? Where did you get this from?"

Shaw flopped down into the chair, exhausted. At this point he might as well tell her everything.

Detective Hall gathered up the other photos and spread them all out on the table, comparing the crimes. She raised a hand to her mouth, then turned to face her colleague and wait for an explanation.

"It's a case from twenty years ago," Shaw said, no longer seeing the point in keeping it secret anymore. But he was still reluctant to dig into every little detail of what he had been up to.

"Why didn't you say something to me before?" asked Jane, blinking furiously and glancing back and forth from the pictures to Eric. They usually shared everything they knew about cases with each other, and it was normal that his behavior would confuse her.

"I wasn't sure about it," he lied. "Not until I connected Garnish to the case."

"Is Garnish involved in these murders too?" She was barely able to contain her surprise.

Eric shrugged. "There's not enough proof to convict him. Back then he was interrogated because he worked at a nearby house, but there was no reason to think he was actually directly involved."

"But the Black Death cases are connected to him! This changes everything!" Jane couldn't stop looking at the photographs.

"Yes, in theory. But we need physical proof; otherwise our hands are tied."

Jane flopped down in the other chair as if Eric's fatigue were contagious. "Something doesn't add up," she said, a perplexed furrow forming on her brow. "Okay, these crimes look a lot alike, but what does the murder of Daniel Pennington have to do with them?"

Eric's cell phone rang, and he took it out of his pocket to answer. "Shaw."

"Boss, Gordon here, from down at the garage," said an excited voice on the line.

As soon as the elevator doors opened, Eric came racing out and headed straight across the atrium. "Miriam!" he shouted as he went.

She was standing just outside the entryway, watching Garnish walk across the well-lit courtyard toward the main gate, accompanied by his lawyer.

Miriam's head spun around quickly when she heard his tone of voice.

"We found the weapon!" shouted Shaw, running toward her. "Stop him immediately!"

Miriam looked confused for a fraction of a second, almost as if she needed a moment to absorb the meaning of his words. Then she turned back toward Garnish, pulling her gun from its holster with her right hand and pointing it across the courtyard. "Stop right there!" she yelled, running toward their suspect.

Garnish's expression was twisted by anger. The lawyer stepped aside immediately once the detective reached them, her gun aimed steadily at his client.

"Hey, darling," said Christopher, outwardly calm. "No need to get all worked up. I'm not going anywhere." His eyes moved to meet Eric's, who was just now coming up behind Miriam. Then, with a swift, sudden movement, Garnish grabbed Miriam by her right wrist, yanking her between himself and Shaw.

"No!" shouted Eric, pointing his own gun at Garnish.

Garnish punched Miriam in the face, sending her reeling, and took advantage of her confusion by grabbing her gun and pulling the woman in close to use as a shield. He raised his right hand and drove the barrel of the pistol into her temple, hugging her close with his other arm.

Eric groaned inwardly. That's where he'd heard that voice. An image of the man who had attacked Adele the other night outside the pub began to take shape in his mind. He was holding Miriam the same way. The voice was the same voice.

Even more enraged than before, Eric took two steps forward, pointing his gun threateningly at the criminal.

"You sure you want to do this?" challenged Garnish. "You have to be sure you're going to hit me and not her." He put his head even closer to Detective Leroux's, making her grimace. A line of blood threaded its way down her cheek from the corner of her mouth.

There was shouting in the distance. Police officers were running toward them from all directions. Christopher glanced quickly left and right, evaluating his next move.

"Give up. You know there's no way out," said Eric. In reality, he was afraid the criminal would drag Miriam out through the open gate, which was directly behind him, but unless Garnish happened to have a car parked and waiting for him just outside, he couldn't possibly get very far.

His lawyer had backpedaled and stood with his back against the fence, watching the scene unfold and doing everything he could to get involved as little as possible. He certainly didn't seem willing to help his client break the law.

The corners of Garnish's mouth turned up. "I'll kill the whole lot of you, one by one!" His tone was cold and resolute—the sound of a man who didn't have anything left to lose. "And as for you," he growled, pulling Miriam tighter and placing his mouth at her ear. "I'll take care of you soon enough, my beautiful little Frenchie."

Suddenly Garnish shoved Miriam into Shaw, sending him stumbling and blocking his view.

Eric grabbed her to keep her from falling, and by the time he looked up again, the criminal had already dashed out through the gate and was running across the street.

Just then, the first pair of officers caught up with them. Miriam pulled away from Eric and took a gun from the first officer who reached them. Weapon in hand, she took off after their fugitive.

"Not again!" Eric groaned, then reluctantly took off after her.

Christopher had already reached the far side of the street and had a decent head start. Suddenly he spun around and fired a shot in their direction. Miriam and Eric ducked, slowing down.

"Fils de chienne!" swore Miriam as a passerby threw herself to the ground, terrorized, and other pedestrians went running in all directions. She set off after Christopher even faster than before.

Eric was struggling to keep up with her. Two chases in one day was at least one too many. Suddenly he realized they were near the St. James's Park station. "If he gets down into the tube, we'll lose him!"

In fact, that was exactly what Christopher had in mind. He ran headlong into the first entrance to the station, disappearing from view, followed a moment later by Miriam.

Eric made it to the entrance too, but when he was inside all he could see was an enormous crowd. He skidded to a stop and craned his neck, looking around for the other two. Finally he caught sight of Miriam, who was running up the stairs to the Circle line. "Police!" she cried, waving people out of the way.

Eric jumped over the turnstiles, but as soon as he made it to the top of the stairs, he could see that Garnish was already down at the bottom, heading into the corridors. He decided to keep Miriam in sight while he elbowed his way through the crowd, trying to get downstairs as quickly as possible. They all kept running. His breath was getting shorter and shorter. He wasn't even sure where he was, but sooner or later they'd reach a platform and that bastard would have nowhere left to run.

There he was! Eric could see a train waiting beyond Garnish, its doors open. It was about to leave. He could hear the door alarms beeping.

Miriam was ahead of him and had almost reached the closing door, but she was a split second too late and it closed. "No!" she shouted, pounding on the window while the passengers stared out at her, their mouths open in surprise. Garnish was standing among them, smiling and waving good-bye to her with one hand.

Eric reached Miriam as the train was pulling away. She gave a deep growl of frustration, then spun around and kicked a trash can in anger, denting it.

Shaw fell to his knees, struggling to breathe. His mind was racing as he tried to figure out what to do next. They'd lost their suspect. There was no way to tell where he was headed. He could get anywhere from here.

Or could he? He needed to think . . .

"Garnish has been watching us for a while," Eric muttered, his voice choked.

"What?" exclaimed Miriam, whirling around. Her face was bright red, and she couldn't stand still—she was shaking her head, struggling with her usual tic.

"I saw him outside the pub the night of Jane's party," Shaw said.

Miriam stopped moving suddenly, all ears. He had her undivided attention.

"This afternoon, just a few hours before I noticed him outside my building, I saw him following me." He stopped and took a long, deep breath. His heart was finally slowing down a little. "Only I didn't know it was him."

"Is he out to get us?" asked Miriam, incredulous. The weapon she was holding trembled with each muscle spasm. "Or just you?"

Eric shook his head. "I don't know." Of course he knew that sooner or later his bad reputation among criminals might come home to roost, but he still found it hard to believe that this whole situation had resulted from his questionable tactics. For now, though, it was the only explanation that made any sense.

Miriam froze, staring Eric straight in the eye. "He tried to attract your attention by copycatting murders committed twenty years ago."

Eric felt short of breath again. She had noticed the connection too. Of course she had. And she hadn't had the courage to bring it up again either. Eric nodded. He'd thought it might be a personal message too. "This man is psychotic." It was the only response he could muster.

"But . . . what about the Pennington murder?" asked Miriam. Then her face lit up with understanding.

Eric had come to the same conclusion. "You heard it too. He said that he'd kill us all." He took in Miriam's dumbfounded look for a few moments, but she didn't say a thing.

"Daniel Pennington was collateral damage," Shaw said, finally breaking the silence. As soon as he said that, he could feel fear rising up inside his chest. "He was looking for someone else—someone who lived at the address until just a little while ago and who is still listed as a resident there."

"Adele," moaned Miriam. "*Your* Adele!"

"Jesus, he's headed for her!" Eric spun around and looked up at the train timetables. "The next train leaves in seven minutes. Too long!"

"We'll take my car!" exclaimed Miriam, running back toward the exit.

She put on the safety glasses and ear protection, then loaded the weapon.

She'd done this hundreds of times and moved automatically, but never before had it been so fundamentally important to follow procedure down to the letter. She was holding the only ironclad proof that connected Garnish with the murders. His prints were the only ones on the gun. If the bullets gathered in the four murder cases could be connected to this gun, it would be enough to put the man behind bars.

"One shot," announced Jane, pointing the pistol into the box. A moment later she pulled the trigger.

The sound of the shot echoed around the ballistics lab, while the bullet penetrated into the gel and came to a stop a little more than halfway through the block.

The criminologist extracted the bullet and set it beneath the microscope. Then she repeated the procedure, this time with the silencer equipped, since it might affect the marks the barrel made on the bullet.

He was clinging to the handle above the car window with one hand while holding his cell phone to his ear with the other.

Next to him Miriam was driving full throttle, sirens blaring, accelerating whenever she had a chance, and slamming on the brakes or swerving to one side whenever they came upon some obstacle. "Get out of the way, you *idiot*!" she shouted at another driver, whose only fault was to have stopped at a stoplight.

On the other end, the phone continued to ring. Suddenly someone picked up . . . but it was just the answering machine. "Fuck!" shouted Eric. "Adele! Don't go to my apartment; go back to the office. I repeat: don't go to my apartment! As soon as you get this, call me. Immediately!" He hung up and dialed another number as quickly as he could. On the fifth ring, his own answering machine message came on. She wasn't there or wasn't able to answer. His mind filled with terror, he managed to make a third call.

The cell phone ringtone was that of a drumroll. Martin, sitting in front of his computer, reached out and touched the screen, answering with the speakerphone.

"Let's see that image again," said Jane, who was standing behind him.

"Stern here," said Martin, distractedly.

"Trace Adele's cell phone with the GPS, immediately!" shouted Eric. They could hear sirens blaring in the background, as well as the engine of Miriam's car roaring.

"Eric?" said Detective Hall.

"Immediately!"

"Yessir." Martin started typing away on his keyboard.

"We checked Garnish's gun against the bullets we gathered in the other cases," continued Jane. "It's a match. He's not getting away this time."

"We have to catch him first," said Shaw, his voice nearly drowned out by a honking horn.

"Where the heck are you?" asked Jane. He'd run out of the building, but she had no idea where he'd gone.

"We think Garnish is going after Adele."

"What!" Jane was incredulous. What the hell was happening? Why would Garnish go after Adele?

Stern stopped moving, drawing Hall's attention to the image on his screen. "Um, boss . . . here it looks like Adele's cell phone is . . . in y-your apartment." Martin was stammering as if he'd said something he wasn't supposed to.

However, the location on the screen made Jane smile. "What's Adele doing at your house, boss?"

"It's not what it looks like," said Eric curtly. Then he hung up.

"To me it looks like you two have gotten together," said Jane to no one in particular, amused at her discovery.

His heart in his throat, Eric ran up the stairs two at a time until he reached his floor. When he came around the corner and could see the door to his apartment, he skidded to a stop. It was open slightly.

Miriam came running up behind him, but he waved back at her to be silent.

He took out his cell phone and dialed Adele's number again. A few moments later he heard a phone ring inside his apartment. It was close. This was the worst possible situation they could have found themselves in. If she was in there, she was unable to respond. The open door made him fear the worst.

No. No. He couldn't lose her now, not after they'd finally found one another. A wave of pain cut through his thoughts. He tried to push it away. He refused to believe it. He had to believe he'd gotten here in time.

Eric snapped the cell phone shut and stuck it in his pocket. He took out his gun, and so did Miriam.

They walked cautiously toward the door. Eric stretched out one hand and pushed the door delicately to open it the rest of the way. The hinge squeaked faintly, interrupting a silence that was otherwise complete save for their stifled breathing. He stopped, swearing to himself.

Miriam moved to the other side of the door and leaned over to look in through the crack.

"See anything?" whispered Shaw.

She shook her head, then took a small flashlight out of her pocket and turned it on, pointing it out from the barrel of her gun. Then she gave the door a sharp shove, throwing it wide open. Trying to make as little noise as possible, they entered the apartment one after the other, crossing through the entryway and heading toward the living room.

Eric's eyes were drawn to something. He'd almost stepped on it: Adele's smartphone, abandoned on the floor not far from the door. He looked around. The little table by the front door had been moved slightly, as if it had been bumped.

He kept walking inside. Part of him wanted to stop right there, terrorized at the thought of what he might find in one of the rooms.

The living room, bathed in light from the street lamps outside, looked in order. Detective Leroux leaned her head through another doorway to check the kitchen, leaving Eric with the bedroom.

He swallowed and clenched the grip of his pistol even more tightly. Seen from the entrance, the room looked dark. He took out his flashlight and pointed it ahead, holding it close to the barrel of his gun just like Miriam. He went in. He could see the bed, still mussed up. Something dark on the floor drew his attention, and he pointed the flashlight at it. Adele's big bag.

He stood there for a moment, struggling to catch his breath. Then he flicked the switch and turned on the light. The room was empty.

"I checked Brian's room and the other bathroom too," said Miriam, coming up behind him. "There's nobody here. Did you look in there?" she asked, pointing to the bathroom connected to the master bedroom.

Eric didn't answer. He was still staring at the bed. There was no sign of Adele, but all her things were still here, including her phone. There was only one explanation. "He took her." The mere thought that Garnish may have taken her sent chills down his spine. They could be anywhere by now. How on earth would he find them?

No, wait a minute.

"Nothing," said Miriam, who had checked the last bathroom in the meantime.

There was something missing.

Eric returned his gun to its holster and went back toward the front door. He knelt down and picked up the smartphone. From there he started carefully checking the floor. "Turn on the light," he said to Miriam.

The room became bright.

"What are you looking for?" she asked.

"Did you notice if my car was parked out front?"

"I didn't see . . . ," said Miriam. She wasn't tense the way she had been before, but her anxiety was now revealing itself under the light, her body continuously trembling.

Eric stood up and put his hand on her forearm, blocking her involuntary movements. He couldn't take care of her, not right now. He had to think of Adele.

Miriam met his quiet gaze and nodded as if she'd read his thoughts.

Eric left her there and went back into the living room, but this time he headed straight for the balcony.

Miriam came to his side by the railing. "He came here on the tube," she muttered. "That bastard came here on the tube."

"He stole my car!" Eric took his cell phone out of his pocket and pressed redial. When he heard the click of someone picking up on the other end, he started talking right away, not even waiting for an answer. "Stern, locate the GPS signal on my car. Now. Quickly!"

"We should be close," said Miriam, slowing down her car. "This is the neighborhood."

Following Stern's directions, the two had driven out to an industrial zone on the outskirts of the city. It was now after ten in the evening, and at this hour the wide, identical streets in this corner of the city were all deserted, save for suburban fauna busily rummaging around in the garbage cans.

"There it is!" exclaimed Eric.

Just ahead they could see his SUV parked along the side of the road, outside of a little red brick building. It looked like a warehouse, but one that hadn't been open for a long time.

Without saying a word, Shaw opened the door and practically leapt out of the car, which was still moving.

"Wait!" said Miriam, hitting the brakes. "That place must be enormous. We have to wait for backup." But her voice was already far behind him.

Eric ran across the cracked asphalt and followed the outside walls of the building, looking for a way in. Given that his SUV was parked here, they had to be relatively close by. He turned the corner, headed down a side street that was poorly lit by an old street lamp. The air was channeled down this street, creating a strong current that made the lamp sway slightly. A gray cat appeared out of nowhere, dashing past him from its hiding place. The cat hissed at him as it passed, its tail raised and fur standing on end. Eric feinted a kick at it and the animal took off more quickly than it had appeared, disappearing into the darkness.

When he turned around again toward the wall, he thought he could just make out a dark door a few yards away. He went over and gave it a push. It opened immediately but was blocked halfway open. Eric squeezed in through the gap, holding his gun and flashlight out firmly in both hands.

The beam of light filled the space in front of him with dancing shadows. The warehouse wasn't abandoned at all. The enormous space was filled roughly two-thirds with boxes of all shapes and sizes. It was probably a storage space for valuable stolen merchandise—Garnish's business. The boxes divided the large warehouse into a maze of corridors.

The flash of a reflection drew his attention. There was something metal to the left, a staircase. He pointed his flashlight on it. It led up to a walled-in loft space, also built of metal, that ran along one side of the building all the way to the opposite wall. Originally it must have contained the building's offices.

Eric blinked furiously. Was that a faint light he could see?

He didn't have time to think. He went up the stairs, careful not to make any noise. When he reached the top he turned off the flashlight. Keeping his hand on the wall to his left, he walked slowly forward until he'd reached the other end.

He was right. There was a very faint ray of light filtering out from beneath a door, even though the door was closed. Now he could see it clearly in the surrounding darkness.

He walked over to the door, listening intently. Maybe he should simply charge in with his gun out and then decide what to do from there. He had little concern for his own safety. He had to save Adele. Garnish wanted him—Eric—and that's the way things should be. The thought that he was stepping into a trap made almost no difference to him.

He put his hand on the door. He listened carefully, trying to figure out if there were any sounds emanating from within, but he couldn't hear anything besides the wind outside, which whined through fissures in the walls of the old building.

He turned the handle and pushed the door open, pointing his gun ahead of him, ready to fire. Suddenly it was as if every sound disappeared, sucked out of his consciousness. "Thank God," he murmured in spite of himself.

Adele was sitting in a chair. A thin line of red ran down from her eyebrow, alongside her eye and then over her cheek, terminating in a dangling drop of blood. An ugly bruise stood out on her pale face, coloring her cheekbone. She was shaking her head violently in his direction.

For a moment Eric didn't understand. His instinct was stronger than any reasoning. "Adele!" he exclaimed, walking into the room.

"Good evening," said a voice.

Shaw turned his gun toward the sound just as Christopher Garnish emerged from a dark corner of the office. He was armed too, but his pistol was pointed straight at Adele. It was the gun he'd ripped away from Miriam.

"Whatever shall we do, Detective?" said the criminal, his tone almost conciliatory. "Want to see who's faster?"

Eric wasn't going to be intimidated by this man. "It's over. Reinforcements are already on their way," he said, taking a couple of cautious steps forward.

By way of an answer, Garnish stepped next to the seated woman and put the barrel of his gun to her temple. "Reinforcements?" He laughed. "Like her?" He nodded to Eric's right.

Miriam stepped in through another doorway. "Throw down your weapon!"

"Throw down yours!" said Lorna Dillon from behind Miriam, pointing her own pistol at the back of Miriam's head.

Miriam's face hardened, but she dropped her weapon, letting it slide off her index finger and clatter to the floor, raising up a small puff of dust. The detective slowly raised both hands in the air.

Lorna shoved her forward toward the center of the room, then kicked her pistol away.

Eric's heart rate spiked. He had to figure out a way to get them out of this situation. He was still holding his gun, but the two criminals were threatening both Miriam and Adele. Adele had started breathing heavily, the same way she had that morning when she saw Daniel's body.

Miriam, on the other hand, was as immobile as a wax statue. She wasn't showing even the faintest glimpse of the anxiety she'd displayed in his apartment. Her eyes were fixed on his, concentrated and calm . . . too calm.

"Fuck you!" shouted Miriam suddenly. Her elbow went flying backward, catching Lorna in the ribs and driving her aim off. Miriam spun around in the same movement, grabbing the woman's right wrist and raising it up in the air. Lorna was driven into the wall, her back smacking into the cement with a dull thud.

Garnish raised his gun and shot.

"No!" shouted Eric, while Miriam buckled under the blow.

Miriam loosened her grip on Christopher's companion and fell to the floor.

At that point, Shaw stopped thinking entirely. He aimed at Garnish and fired. Once, then again, hitting the man both times as Lorna began screaming.

The world seemed to have slipped into slow motion. He saw Adele throw herself to the floor and grab Miriam's gun. Lying down, she rolled over, aimed at Dillon, and shot the woman in the head.

A look of utter stupor came over Dillon's face as a gush of blood shot out of a hole in her forehead. Then her body collapsed and slid down the wall alongside Miriam.

A second later the silence was absolute.

Still incredulous, Eric looked around the room, uncertain whether what he was seeing corresponded to the truth. Then Adele yelled out.

He looked at her. She was still holding the gun with which she had shot Lorna. Eric stared into Adele's eyes, horrified by it all.

A sudden sense of urgency drew his attention back to Miriam. She was lying on the floor, motionless.

Eric ran over to her. Her face was covered by her own hair. The bullet wound was in her back, where a large hole had opened up in her leather jacket. He shoved his gun into its holster and touched the wound, then checked his fingers. There was no blood. He reached out again, and only then realized that her back was much more rigid than it should be.

He delicately rolled her over. Her jacket fell open, revealing the bulletproof vest she'd put on. As soon as he saw it, Eric released an enormous sigh of relief. She'd been much more careful than he had.

"How is she?" asked Adele from where she lay on the floor, her voice trembling. She'd abandoned the gun on the floor. She kept her eyes on it, but she was curled up, hugging her knees to her chest.

Shaw touched Miriam's face and laid two fingers on the side of her neck. Her heartbeat was regular. She had simply lost consciousness from the force of the bullet impact. "Hey, wake up," he said quietly, shaking her a little, but she didn't respond.

A deep groan made him turn around.

Garnish was supine on the floor, two large red stains spreading out across his shirt. The blood ran out onto the floor, expanding into a puddle. His body was racked with tremors, his eyes wide open. He was moving one arm in their direction.

This seemed to startle Adele out of her state of shock. "He's still alive . . . ," she murmured, scared but moving toward Garnish.

Eric caressed Miriam's hair. That man had shot her. He didn't deserve Eric's compassion, but deep inside a voice kept telling him he had to do something. Reluctantly he left his "daughter" behind and went over to Garnish.

Adele was kneeling beside the criminal and opening up his shirt. The man's eyes searched hers, begging them. His mouth moved, but he didn't seem capable of producing sound. A bullet wound in the shoulder looked like it wasn't too bad, but the hole in his stomach was losing a lot of blood. The woman looked up and met Eric's eyes. "We have to do something to stop the bleeding."

Eric looked back at her. He was finding it difficult to react to even the slightest stimuli. He could see Adele turning to him for help, but he had no idea what to do. He didn't understand her question.

"Eric!" screamed Adele.

That finally shook Shaw out of his torpor. "There's nothing we can do."

"Goddamn it, call for help! Go on, move!" she yelled at him.

After everything Garnish had done, including murdering her ex-husband less than twenty-four hours ago, Adele was still doing whatever she could to save him.

He felt small and mean for briefly considering letting Garnish bleed to death. Adele was right. He had to call for help.

He pulled his cell phone out of his pocket.

In the meantime, Adele had gone over to Dillon's body and taken the scarf off her neck. She used it to try to stem Christopher's bleeding.

"There's no signal in here," said Eric.

"Go outside. I'll handle this."

He glanced at her, unsure. "Are you sure you'll be okay?"

Adele looked up at him. Her face was calm, the shock that had paralyzed her not long ago now a distant memory. "Yes," she said, displaying a small smile. "Go. I'll wait here for you."

She listened to Eric's footsteps drawing farther away, ringing out as he ran down the metal gangway. It would take him a few minutes to get outside and make the call, longer if he had to go back to Miriam's car and use the radio.

Adele turned to look at Miriam. She was still unconscious. Finally she looked Garnish in the face. Their eyes met and she smiled. Then she took her hand off his wound.

The man's face contorted.

"Don't be afraid," she whispered kindly. "It won't take long. Your life will be over soon."

The man moaned again, stronger than before. "Please . . . ," he managed to whisper in a weak voice.

Adele chuckled. "Who knows how many times you've heard other people say that to you? It sucks to be on the other side, doesn't it?" She leaned in close, bringing her head near his. "You shouldn't have killed Danny too." Then she sat up again and put her hands on the scarf covering his wound; only this time she pressed outward with her fingers, pulling the edges of the wound farther apart.

Garnish emitted a strangled cry as his body contracted, then relaxed. His head rolled to one side, immobile. His eyes were wide open and empty, his mouth half-closed.

Adele felt her own lungs clamoring for air, greedily fighting a growing sense of breathlessness. Tears glistened on her cheeks while her body convulsed with tremors.

A coughing sound made her turn around. Miriam!

She looked at Christopher's body again. She took the scarf off his wound and abandoned it alongside the body. Then she got up.

* * *

He ran up the stairs and across the gangway, but when he got to the door of the office the only thing he found was Garnish's dead body.

"We're over here," said Adele, making him turn on one heel.

Miriam was sitting on the floor, her back against the wall. There was a grimace of pain on her face, but otherwise she seemed okay. At least she was conscious. Adele was kneeling beside her, helping her take off her jacket.

"*Merde! Fais-le lentement!* Be careful . . . ," Miriam said to her.

"Sorry," muttered Adele. "I think she's okay," she said to Eric, irony in her voice.

"What happened to Garnish?" He paused again at the criminal's body. What had happened while he was gone?

"He lost too much blood."

"That son of a bitch must have broken my ribs," said Miriam. "It feels like my chest is being torn apart every time I take a breath."

Adele was opening up her bulletproof vest. There was a bullet lodged in the fabric on the lower part of the vest. "Thank God you were wearing it."

"I don't dash off to play hero without at least a little protection," said Miriam, glaring at Eric.

He went over and knelt down by the two women. He couldn't believe it was over and that they'd managed to get out of it all alive—that he wouldn't be forced to dig into the past.

He looked at Miriam, then Adele.

"Okay, that's good," murmured Dr. Steward to himself as he checked the X-rays. "Just a cracked rib. Nothing serious."

Miriam snorted noisily, then gave a little moan of pain that was swiftly followed by cursing.

"However, you absolutely have to rest," the doctor continued. "For a while you'll feel pain even just taking a deep breath."

"I figured that part out already," she growled.

Adele giggled a little and Detective Leroux cast her a baleful look.

"Don't worry, doctor," said Eric. "We'll take care of her." He gave Miriam's head a swift, paternal caress.

"I'm just sorry I didn't get a chance to watch that bastard die," Miriam said.

The doctor coughed with surprise and gave the other two a perplexed look. "Maybe I can give you something for the pain . . ."

"Bravo. Finally you understand her," said Eric.

But the doctor had already walked away.

Miriam was okay, better than okay in fact. Eric couldn't help but smile when he looked at her. He truly loved her like a daughter. When Garnish had shot her, he'd completely lost control. The mere thought that she might be dead had overwhelmed him. He'd felt a need to annihilate that man. For the first time in his life, he'd been consumed by a thirst for revenge, and he couldn't do anything to stop it. But when he'd seen Garnish lying dead after he'd run outside to call for help, all he'd felt was an enormous emptiness inside.

Part of him was happy the man was dead, but that subtle sense of satisfaction he'd felt when he pulled the trigger had completely vanished.

"Darling!" exclaimed a male voice, dragging Eric back to the present. A big blond man around thirty years old was standing at the door to the hospital room.

"Oh shit! I told you not to come here," said Miriam, clearly annoyed. She buried her face in her hands.

"Are you kidding?" said the young man, going over to her and completely ignoring the other two people in the room. He sat down on the edge of the bed, pulled her hands away from her face, and kissed her passionately.

Eric felt his stomach contract involuntarily. Where the hell had this guy jumped out from? He cleared his throat in an attempt to get their attention, but he had to clear it again, louder this time, before he could get them to pull themselves apart and look at him.

"Um . . . ," said Miriam. She was flustered, something rarely seen in the young detective. "Jonathan, I'd like you to meet Eric and Adele," she said, pointing to them in turn.

"Hi!" said Jonathan, holding out his hand to Eric.

Eric stared at the young man, then down at his hand. He had no intention whatsoever of shaking that thing.

Adele stepped between them, holding her own hand out. "It's a pleasure," she said, smiling. She shot a foot out behind her, kicking Shaw. Reluctantly he stood up and shook Jonathan's hand.

After that, Jonathan only had eyes for his woman, as if the other two had disappeared altogether. He began caressing her face, then her arms, while leaning onto the bed. "Are you sure you're okay, my little darling?"

"I'm fine," said Miriam, almost resigned to his ardent attentions.

"I get the feeling we're two people too many," murmured Adele.

Eric pretended he hadn't heard her and continued to watch the two on the hospital bed. They didn't seem at all like a couple going through a crisis. He suspected that Miriam had exaggerated a little when she'd told him they'd broken up. Or maybe she was just trying to protect her own personal privacy. That thought hurt a little. He'd always looked out for her, protected her, but she'd stopped being a little girl a long time ago.

Now Jonathan was caressing her sides and her stomach, almost as if he wanted to check her out inch by inch. Shaw felt a tug on his arm. He glanced at Adele, perplexed.

"I think they'd like to be *alone*," said Adele, pronouncing her words clearly.

He gave up. She was right. Eric followed Adele out into the hallway. Miriam and Jonathan didn't even appear to notice they were leaving.

Only after he'd gone out through the door and started walking alongside Adele down the hospital corridor did Eric realize just how tired he was. It was after midnight now, and he'd been awake since five o'clock in the morning. He'd just come to the end of what had been his busiest day in decades.

When they stopped outside the elevator, Adele took his hand and glanced up at him furtively. "You're behaving just like a crazy, jealous father," she said.

"I can't help it," said Eric. It was embarrassing to admit.

"It's sweet," said Adele, reaching up and caressing Eric's jawbone with the index finger of her left hand. "I know a secret, something you don't know."

Secret? What secrets were left now? But from the expression on his companion's face, Eric could tell it wasn't bad news.

"I think Miriam is pregnant."

"What!"

"Haven't you noticed how she's got a weak stomach lately, and she's irritable?" Adele paused for a moment, then continued. "Okay, she's always been irritable. But more than usual lately."

Goodness gracious. Yes, he'd noticed. He'd also noticed her panic attacks had returned, after it had seemed like they'd disappeared for good. Now he knew why.

"You're going to be a grandfather . . . Aren't you happy?"

"What! No . . . *No!*" he protested vehemently. A little too vehemently, to be honest. Then he noticed the mocking look in Adele's eyes. "My son is just fifteen years old. I wasn't planning on becoming a grandfather anytime soon."

Adele laughed out loud.

Why the heck was he getting angry? After all, it was good news. Eric started laughing too. Then they both stopped and stared in each other's eyes.

"I think this time I'm going to take at least a week's vacation," Eric said.

"Will you take me up to your country cottage?" She was giving him that naughty young girl glance, the same one that had made him lose control that afternoon.

"I will if you behave," he said, hugging her close. "But first I need to sleep. A lot."

"Let's go home," she whispered in his ear.

The elevator doors rolled open.

"Oh! Hey there!" Jane's voice was unmistakable. This was the last thing they needed right now. "No, no," Jane continued, "I don't want to bother you two." She stepped out of the elevator and brushed past them, pausing only to wink.

CHAPTER 15
SEPTEMBER

"Okay, okay, now it's time for my present!" exclaimed Miriam, plopping a red gift down on the tabletop right in front of Eric.

Today was his birthday, and he'd brought together his entire odd family for dinner: his son, his "adopted" daughter, and his partner Adele. Despite the way their love affair had begun, it was slowly but surely moving forward, with highs and lows and not too much pressure. They'd decided to start by dating, each living at home but taking increasing advantage of opportunities to spend time together and share one another's interests. They wanted to take time to get to know one another and figure out where they were heading together. If he were being completely honest with himself, Eric felt ready to skip a few steps in this process, but he appreciated her attempts to set limits. This way he felt like he appreciated each individual moment more, which was exactly what they had gathered together to do today.

Now looking around and seeing himself surrounded with the people he loved the most, Eric felt truly happy. Though he wasn't the least bit excited to be turning fifty. Surrounded by all these younger people, he felt a little younger himself—and that's exactly what amused his companions the most.

He examined the present with an air of suspicion. He picked it up. It felt light. He shook it but couldn't hear any telltale sounds from within. Whatever lay inside the packaging, it was lodged in tight.

"Go on, open it!" urged Brian.

Adele caressed his arm and looked at him with one of her usual enigmatic smiles.

"How come I've got the feeling that everybody knows what's in here except me?"

"Eric," protested Miriam, "stop being an investigator for once and open that goddamned present!"

Shaw raised both hands in a show of surrender, making everyone there laugh, save Miriam, who stood at his side and glared at him, her hands on her belly, which was just starting to show. *His* baby girl was about to become a mother herself. It was hard for him to think of her in that role, and he continued to be less than impressed with her boyfriend. When she'd told him she would be coming alone because Jonathan had to work, he hadn't exactly broken down in tears. He smiled now at that thought, but Miriam's impatient look told him that now was not the time to make her wait any longer.

Eric untied the bow and started opening the present, moving with deliberate, studied slowness. Every once in a while he stopped, made a silly grimace, and then started again. Finally he got all the wrapping paper off and found himself holding a box with a smartphone.

"Oh no, not one of these infernal contraptions!" he groaned.

"Oh Dieu, le gentil vieil homme . . . ," echoed Miriam, making everyone assembled burst out laughing.

"I'm right here, young lady," he said. "I can hear you, and I can understand you!"

Miriam finally abandoned her grumpy air and smiled, then gave him a gigantic hug. "Happy birthday!" she said, accompanied with a big kiss on the cheek.

Eric took the phone out of its packaging and began examining it suspiciously.

Brian yanked it out of his grip. "You stick your SIM card in here," he said, pointing to the battery slot, which was empty. He pulled out the battery from its box and removed the back cover for his dad. "Then you close it."

Gee whiz, he thought. The kid could already set up a smartphone. "Okay, I think I can take it from here," said Eric.

"No, wait. I still have to show you how to set up your e-mail account."

"Who picked that phone, you or him?" said Eric to Miriam.

Miriam and Adele exchanged a mysterious look. Then Adele said, "To be honest, Jane was the one who suggested it."

"Oh no. That means she must be preparing a trick of some sort for Saturday."

The two women giggled together, obviously accomplices. It was a pleasure to see them like this. They'd never really gotten along together, but over the past few months, once Miriam finally accepted the reality of Eric's relationship with Adele, they'd practically become friends.

"Don't worry. I'm sure the party Jane's preparing will be a relaxed, easygoing affair," said Adele. But her reassuring tone did nothing but raise his innate sense of anxiety. What the heck did she have in mind?

"You know Jane," he said, followed by the sound of their laughter.

Later on he wound up alone in the car with his son. He was bringing the boy back home and wanted to take advantage of the opportunity to have a heart-to-heart with him. Lately that seemed all but impossible to organize, since there were always other people around. Even now, when they were theoretically "alone," that wasn't really the case. Brian was busy messaging someone on his phone and appeared entirely consumed by his virtual conversation.

Lord how the boy had grown over the past few months! When the days slipped past one at a time, it was impossible to see the way they grew up, but seeing him just twice a month made the changes obvious. He'd be turning sixteen soon. He was an adolescent now, and Crystal certainly had her hands full raising him. Being a *good* parent, the one who hands out presents and has all the fun, was something of an advantage. But if he was honest with himself, Eric had to admit that he often missed parenting full time. He had the feeling that he'd lost control of his son's life, and that the person now sitting next to him was becoming more and more of a stranger.

Suddenly Brian burst out laughing. They were stopped at a stoplight, so Eric watched his son sidelong, taking advantage of the opportunity to get a good look at him, his face illuminated by the city lights. There was something in his eyes, a certain kind of mischievousness that Eric knew all too well.

"Who? Nicole?" Obviously he was messaging a girl. That was the only kind of subject that could get Brian to disappear entirely from the world around him like this.

Brian's face reddened, and he shook his head no. It wasn't Nicole.

"So it's someone else, another girl?"

His son fumbled around with his phone, then showed his father a photograph. It was a close-up of a pretty girl with blond hair and green eyes.

"Very pretty!"

The streetlight turned green and the car got moving again.

"Her name is Claudie. She's French."

"Really? Then I'm guessing your French is improving."

"Yeah. Thanks to her. We met on Facebook."

"Oh," was all Eric could reply, taking the opportunity to make a mental note that he should get one of those accounts too. Maybe that way he'd be able to maintain a closer relationship with his son. The thought made him laugh a little to himself. "So you two have never met in person?"

"Well, no. But we've seen each other on Skype."

"Oh." Okay, at least he knew what Skype was, but it would probably be better to change the subject before they wound up in entirely unfamiliar territory.

"She's coming to London on vacation for New Year's Eve." He could tell his son was excited about it. He really liked this girl.

"So she helped you with your French, you said?"

"Yeah. She's really patient. She showed me a ton of websites and interesting blogs where I can practice."

"I like blogs." When they'd started becoming trendy, Eric had followed a few, back when they were a lot more intimate. People wrote about themselves then, protected by anonymity. Those days were nothing like today's social networks. The fact that they'd been anonymous helped people express what they were thinking honestly, directly, and readers all pitched in with advice. He'd found it to be an interesting way to observe humanity. Now blogs had become first and foremost a marketing tool, and they'd lost their original appeal with him.

"There's this one that's really cool," Brian said before his phone beeped again, interrupting the conversation. He typed in a response to his friend with an incredibly rapid dance of fingertips across the screen. "You'd like it," he continued. "It's all about murder."

Eric couldn't help but laugh, which obviously annoyed Brian a tiny bit. "Sorry, sorry," said Eric. "It was just the way you said it. I work with this stuff every day, you know."

"Yeah, but this one's special. At first it seemed like a real story, but then we realized it was all too over the top to be true. It's like a novel about a serial killer."

"It keeps getting better and better," said Eric. There was irony in his voice, but Brian didn't seem to pick up on it.

"It's written by this killer who murders the people who destroyed her family, then frames one of them for the murders she's committed."

What?

"Unfortunately she stopped posting three months ago, just when things were heating up. She'd hidden the murder weapon in this guy's car and then ran away.

Eric hit the brakes. He stared out at the road ahead while a thousand different thoughts raced around in his head. Adrenaline was coursing through his veins, keeping him from moving.

"Dad, what's going on?" Brian reached over and shook his arm gently. "You okay?"

The car behind them started honking, so Eric pulled his SUV over to the side of the road.

He turned to look at his son. "Was . . . When . . . Was the blog in French?" he stammered.

"Yeah, it was . . . What's the matter?"

"Who is the blogger?"

The boy shrugged. "Who knows what her real name is. She signed her posts *Mina*."

"Fuck me . . . ," muttered Shaw. He'd heard the name in his head even before it came out of his son's mouth. He was breathing too quickly. He needed to calm himself down. Maybe it was all just a coincidence. "Where does the story take place?" he asked Brian. He wasn't entirely sure he wanted to hear the answer, but Eric knew he wouldn't be able to rest until he'd found out more. Surely it was an anonymous case. A story like that wasn't really very original. There were probably lots of examples in books and movies.

"Here in London," his son said.

Eric closed his eyes, fighting a feeling that the world was crashing down around him.

"Here, I'll show you." Brian took his tablet out of his backpack. "It's saved in my favorites." He quickly opened his browser and jumped straight to the blog. "Look," he said, holding the tablet up so his father could see.

Eric was almost afraid to take it. Finally he reached out, took the tablet, and started reading. Almost instantly, he was hooked. He ran down the pages, trying to understand the meaning of the French words.

"It's not easy to understand," said Brian. "Claudie had to help me a little." He leaned over to see where his father was in the blog. "If I'd known you were interested in it, I would have told you about it earlier. You could ask Miriam to help you translate it."

"Leave Miriam out of this!" shouted Eric. His son stared at him, open-mouthed and confused. "I'm sorry," he said, trying to calm down. "It's not you. Listen, can you e-mail me a link to this site?"

"Yeah, of course." Brian couldn't hide his curiosity. "What's up? Why won't you tell me what it is?"

Eric took a long, deep breath. He didn't want to scare his son. "I'm sorry," he said. "It's nothing. Probably nothing. It's just some . . . nothing. It reminds me of an old story I read a while back, that's all."

Eric went into his office and locked the door behind him. At this hour, the building was practically deserted, but he wanted to make sure he wouldn't be disturbed. Someone, Jane for example, might find it strange to see him in here working on his birthday. He certainly would have preferred to spend the evening somewhere else, but he couldn't put this off.

He turned on his computer and waited patiently for it to warm up. It always seemed too slow when he really needed it. One last glance out of the glass door to the office. No lights, no noises.

Eric opened his e-mail and saw the message from Brian. He clicked on the link and found himself staring at the blog.

Mina's Blog.

That was the title. Simple, straightforward. It looked like any other website, equipped with minimalist, welcoming graphics. But the content froze his blood. Evidently it didn't have the same effect on its numerous subscribers, who left plenty of commentary after the entries, evidently believing them nothing more than very convincing stories. But for Eric, they were far more than that.

Every detail checked out. In the sections where his rusty French, learned thanks to his close connection with Miriam and her extended family, wasn't good enough, he cut and pasted segments into Google Translate.

With every line, every paragraph, all the little pieces of the puzzle fell into place. All the little inconsistencies he'd spent so much time trying to ignore suddenly became too much to push away.

He knew it. He'd always known that *she* must have been involved, but he'd never wanted to believe it. Garnish had been too enticing a lead to let go, and his death had been far too convenient. The truth of this case died along with Christopher Garnish, and that had been enough for Eric, at least until now.

Now that he found himself faced with the cynicism in those words, with the complete and utter absence of remorse, with Mina's wickedness and malice, Eric couldn't lie to himself any longer.

He still hoped that somehow he was wrong. After all, what was he looking at? A blog? A work of fiction? But no. He was sure she was the author . . . The details were too precise, too accurate. She hadn't even hidden the names with pseudonyms. She must have been completely sure no one would ever make the connection. Or maybe she wasn't afraid it would happen. It was just supposed to be a story. If it had been something different, she would undoubtedly have erased it already. Why leave clues behind her? Why, after she'd spent so much time and energy carrying out the perfect vendetta?

Unless she wanted to leave crumbs, wanted to be discovered. There were only a very few people on the planet who could connect that blog, that name, to the real facts. Eric might well be the only person who had all the information necessary to do so.

He released the breath he'd been involuntarily holding back. No. It couldn't be true. They were certain a man was involved in those murders. They had the video from outside the building where the first victim was murdered. The fake woman dressed in black was undoubtedly a man. It couldn't be her.

He typed in his password to access the evidence online and watched the video.

There was the person dressed in black, walking into the building. The gait was awkward, the shoulders too large for the hips. It had to be a man. Little Sayyid had seen that person walk out of the victim's apartment that same day. The same clothing with traces of blood from Thompson, McKinsey, and Ridley had been found in Garnish's car. The blog didn't talk about that clothing directly.

He fast-forwarded the video until he saw the person in black leave the building twenty minutes later. The same awkward gait. The killer moved toward the video camera.

That was strange. The killer left in the opposite direction from which he—or she—had arrived.

Once the figure in black disappeared, Eric's gaze was drawn to a young man walking behind the killer, all the way at the end of the frame. He had a courier company's logo on his jacket and was carrying a package under one arm. He was wearing a baseball cap down tight on his head.

He stopped the video, then ran it backward as slowly as he could.

At a certain point the young man seemed to pop up out of nowhere behind the figure dressed in black.

"What the hell . . . ?"

He backed up to the point where the suspect walked out through the building's main door, then forward just one frame at a time. The camera angle was set in such a way that it covered the view of the entrance for a number of seconds. The young man appeared immediately after the suspect walked out.

He'd come from inside the building.

He rewound the video again. If the young man had come out of that building, then at some point he must have gone in too.

No one had entered the building during the twenty minutes that passed from when the figure in black had gone in and when he or she came out again. A number of different people had walked past on the sidewalk: a mother and her child, a teenage couple . . . No one had so much as glanced at the entrance to that building.

He reached the point where the figure in black went in, then continued until he saw the killer disappear from the top corner of the image. But he didn't stop there. He ran the video back for a few more minutes until another figure appeared in the doorway, walking backward across the screen.

The courier.

The courier came from the same direction he went when he left, but he was holding the same package. Why hadn't he dropped it off? He'd gone in, stayed inside for more than twenty minutes, then left again carrying what appeared to be the same package.

They'd been so focused on that bizarre figure dressed in black from head to toe that they'd completely ignored a classic clue that should have jumped off the screen to any investigator.

He froze the image. The courier looked like a young man. He was wearing jeans and a puffy jacket. He had a pair of dark sunglasses on beneath his cap and kept his head low. It was just barely possible to make out his chin and lower lip.

Eric tried to zoom the image, but the details were blurry and didn't reveal anything that might make the person more recognizable.

He went back to the full picture, enlarged the entire screen, and started analyzing it frame by frame, looking for something. Not even Eric was sure exactly what.

At a certain point his attention was drawn to the package. It was a cardboard box with a label stuck on top, but it was impossible to read what was written on the label. The courier kept the package tucked against his chest with his left hand.

Eric turned the zoom back on, pulling in until a hand and forearm filled up the entire screen. The resolution wasn't the best, but he could see well enough.

He felt tears well up in his eyes. What was he supposed to do now?

He turned the key in the lock slowly, trying not to make any noise. He didn't usually go in like this without knocking when he knew she was at home. But if he'd rung the bell at this hour of the night, he would only scare her, and that's not what he wanted to do. He preferred to surprise her before confronting her. Eric had no idea how all this would end. All he felt was an unstoppable desire to have the truth out on the table. He wanted clarity. The only thing that counted now was the truth; he'd worry about the consequences later.

He opened the door a crack and listened. The room was filled with dim lamplight. He could hear water running in the background. He went in and closed the door gently behind him. She was taking a shower, so she couldn't have heard him come in.

Eric swallowed. He couldn't do anything but wait. That seemed easy enough, but his nervousness was killing him. Every passing second made the wait more difficult. Images of the victims filled his mind, flanked by images of little Mina. How could that young girl have turned into such a merciless monster?

Deep in his heart, Eric felt responsible. He knew he shouldn't, but a small, wormlike sense of guilt kept winding its way through his mind. That was the reason why he hadn't mentioned his suspicions and discoveries to anyone, and it was the reason why he still hadn't decided what he was going to do. He kept telling himself that first and foremost he wanted to understand. But what was there to understand, really? His mind could barely conceive of those facts, those acts, and no justification would be enough to clear them. Yet somehow he still kept hoping there might be something that would make everything right again.

A quick whirring noise made him start and turn around. The fan on the notebook computer sitting on the table had fired up.

Maybe he should look for a little more information before he talked to her.

He walked over to the computer and brushed his fingers across the touchpad. The screensaver disappeared and the access window popped up in its place, asking for the password. Without even thinking about it, he sat down and typed in "19940403." April 3, 1994: the day Mina's family had been brutally massacred.

As soon as he hit return, the desktop opened up on the screen. The background was a photo of the two of them together, taken not more than a month ago. The pairing of that image and the date he'd used to get into the computer gave Eric the chills. Icons kept popping up, one after another. Soon the screen was almost entirely covered. They'd been arranged in such a way that they covered up the faces in the background. In addition to the usual computer program icons, there were a number he didn't recognize. It took him a little while to find the documents folder.

He stopped. He thought he heard noises in the other room. He waited a few moments, then the water started running again.

He took a deep breath to calm himself and then opened the folder, finding a myriad of subfolders inside. What on earth did he think he was doing? Was he really going to check them all, one by one? He certainly didn't have enough time. It looked like she catalogued everything. There was a folder for every case she'd ever worked on, along with others for photographs, music, film, and so forth. Knowing her, he'd expected things to be better organized. But that was precisely the point, wasn't it: Did he really know her?

He ran the cursor down the sidebar. Then his eyes fell on a folder titled, simply, "Eric." He felt nauseated for a moment, but he had to open it. Inside were other subfolders, divided by year starting in 2000. He double-clicked on the year 2000 and found himself looking at an amazing number of images. He could see from the thumbnails that some were scanned newspaper articles. Opening one by chance, he saw that it was the story of a murder case. His name was mentioned in the article heading. It was the same with the others.

There were photographs too, several hundred of them, showing him on the street or at the scene of a crime, going into or coming out of his apartment building. Eric felt his stomach turn over.

Gripped with a growing sense of anxiety, Eric moved on to another year. It was filled with the same kinds of files—only there were a lot more this time. There were more and more each year, until he came to the preceding year. There was no folder for the current year.

She'd started keeping tabs on him back when she was still a young girl. Every cell in his body screamed for him to get out of there, to go as far away as possible. He was angry, and he felt stupid for never having picked up on any of this, but he had to keep going forward. Mina's morbid fascination with him didn't prove anything. He was looking for something else entirely on that computer.

He went back to the documents folder and kept scrolling down until he found a subfolder with the name "Garnish." Inside were other subfolders divided by year, this time starting from 2010. Photographs taken secretly in a range of different circumstances. Some showed the man in the company of Thompson, McKinsey, Ridley, and Dillon, though the people were always with Garnish separately, never all together. There was even a folder containing copies of the police reports for each of them, apparently taken from the archives. He found the oldest one of all in there, the one containing details of the massacre that had occurred twenty years earlier, which had been just another interrogation for him.

Somehow Mina had reconnected all the information. Unlike Eric, she had the advantage of having been there when the crime was committed. She had seen the men who murdered her family with her own eyes. Back then they hadn't even considered interrogating her because she'd been too young and in complete shock. They'd assumed she'd hidden when it started and hadn't seen a thing. Besides, who would have believed the word of a seven-year-old girl who'd just seen her family brutally murdered? They weren't even sure she was capable of understanding what had happened, much less identifying those responsible. They had completely underestimated her.

Here was the proof he'd been looking for.

Out of the corner of his eye he saw movement in the doorway to the bedroom.

She was standing there, pointing a pistol at his head. "Jesus Christ, Eric!" she said, lowering the gun. "What the hell are you doing here? I thought you were a thief!"

Eric stood up slowly from the chair, finding it hard to breathe. He'd been so completely concentrated on the files on the computer that he hadn't heard the shower turning off.

She stared at him, sensing something was wrong. She was barefoot and wearing a pair of gray pajamas. Her hair was wet. The gun was still in her left hand, but now she lowered it down at her side. Her eyes moved from his face to the open notebook computer on the table, and then her expression hardened.

"What are you doing on my computer?" she demanded, her voice little more than a whisper. She seemed perplexed, but there was a vaguely accusatory tone in her voice. Her hand tightened on her weapon while her eyes searched Eric.

Detective Shaw sighed. The moment had come. "I remember that day, last January, when you came to visit me in my office."

He'd heard a knock on the door, and then it opened. The first thing he'd seen was her brown hair, shining faintly auburn in the sunlight streaming in through the window. And her beautiful green eyes.

"Good morning, boss. Can I talk to you for a couple of minutes?"

"Adele Pennington, right?"

She'd been assigned to his team merely two days earlier. He'd met her briefly, but they hadn't started working together yet.

Adele nodded.

"Please, come on in. Make yourself comfortable." Eric, sitting at his desk, waved to the chairs set up on the other side.

"I think I'll stand, thanks."

"What can I do for you, Miss Pennington?"

The woman had smiled. That was the first time he'd noticed her smile. He remembered thinking she really was beautiful, more striking than any of his colleagues. But maybe that was just because she was so young. How old was she? Twenty-six, twenty-seven at most.

Adele hesitated for a moment, apparently embarrassed. "I just felt I should tell you, before we start working together, that we've already met. But I'm sure you don't recognize me now."

Eric furrowed his brow and stared at her, interested. They already knew each other? He doubted it. He would never have forgotten a woman like this. "To be honest, I don't think I've ever met an Adele Pennington in my life. But it's true that this job puts me into contact with lots of different people, and sometimes I don't recognize them when I should." He felt bad that he didn't recognize her.

The young woman smiled. "No, it's been a long time. I was just a young girl. When we met I had another name." She paused, and the tension between them grew. She had the detective's complete attention. "Adelmine Fontaine."

In a fraction of a second Eric saw the image of that young girl he'd found at the scene of the crime twenty years earlier materializing in his mind. She had the same eyes that he now saw in the young woman standing in front of him. "Mina . . . ," murmured Eric, incredulous.

Back at the apartment, he must have spoken out loud, because Adele nodded.

"I was sure you'd figure it out sooner or later, reading the file. I just thought I should be the one to tell you." Adele's fingers danced along the hilt of her gun. She didn't appear to have any intention of putting it down.

"You only did so because, if I'd discovered on my own by chance, you thought I wouldn't have appreciated it." Eric kept his eyes on her hand, but he couldn't help the stern tone in his voice. "What's more, you did everything you could to make sure I'd notice. I have to admit you did a good job."

Ever since he'd been aware that this woman was the same little girl he'd found in the most gruesome case he'd ever worked on, he couldn't help but feel curious about her. What had she been doing all these years? Against his better judgment, this curiosity had evolved into an even deeper interest in her as a woman, an interest that made Eric deeply uncomfortable. It seemed inappropriate somehow to feel that way about a person he'd met when she was just a seven-year-old girl. The worst part was that the more he admitted his feelings, the more attracted to her he felt.

"I don't usually go digging around in my colleagues' pasts, but of course I would have noted the coincidence in the names. Adelmine isn't exactly a household name, but that wouldn't have been enough to make me think you were the same person. The last name is different."

The woman smiled faintly. "You're an intelligent man. Sooner or later you would have figured it out."

He still hadn't accused her of anything, but they were already laying their cards out on the table. This worried him, because Adele was the one holding a gun in her hand.

"Of course I didn't think you were married. Back then I guess I just assumed they had adopted you."

"I grew up with my maternal grandparents here in London. They raised me, but I kept my last name."

"That's why you couldn't wait to get a new one, and why you kept the new one even after your divorce." Eric was only now realizing that this woman had spent the last twenty years planning and organizing her life in such a way that she could get to him and the men who had murdered her family. Every decision, every choice she'd made, had been directed to that end.

Adele's face darkened. "I thought of Danny as my family!" she exclaimed, raising her voice a little. Then she took a deep breath and regained control of herself. "He lived in the house next door to my grandparents. He was my first friend, the first friend I made after I moved there. My only friend. I spent more time over at his house than anywhere else." Her eyes reddened and a tear trickled down her left cheek. She reached up and nervously rubbed her free hand across her face to dry it. "I envied him a little because he still had his parents. I wanted to be his sister. I wanted his parents to become my parents." Her words were choked with emotion. It was almost as if she felt guilty for things she'd felt as a young girl. "But I really, truly loved him. And he loved me."

"Enough to become your accomplice," he said. Now was the time to strike, while she was weak. "I imagine you told him what happened to you, back when you were still kids. And he promised you he would help you take revenge for your family." Eric gave a short, bitter laugh. "I'll bet you were already a talented manipulator back then. And your skills only improved with practice." He shook his head, still incredulous despite the evidence lying before him. "You even managed to manipulate me.

You started the day we met, and you never stopped since, not even for a moment. You're still trying to manipulate me even now!"

Adele's emotions seemed to disappear in an instant. She dropped her mask. Her gaze turned hard again, but she still didn't say anything. She would never confess, he was sure of it. She was studying him, trying to figure out if he could hurt her, and in order to do that she would wait patiently to hear what he had to say next.

"He was the figure dressed in black," said Eric, referring to Daniel Pennington. "You used him to draw attention away from yourself. He was like a spotlight directed out into the audience, while you changed the scenery onstage." He scrutinized the woman standing before him, but she didn't so much as blink. "You wanted him to be noticed. You wanted us to figure out he was a man. That way you could lay the blame on Garnish."

This time he thought he could make out the tiniest bit of satisfaction in Adele's expression, but it came and went too quickly for him to be sure. She couldn't keep pretending she was indifferent forever.

"I have proof you were there," Eric added.

Adele opened and closed her eyes repeatedly. That revelation appeared to surprise her. She was obviously wondering whether or not it was true. Maybe she was mentally reexamining her steps, trying to see where she'd slipped up. Then she smiled again. "You don't have a thing," she said, sounding completely sure of herself. She was convinced she hadn't made any mistakes.

"I saw you in the video."

She didn't react but challenged him with her eyes.

"Oh, your courier outfit was perfect. Not to mention the way you misled the video feed, walking out of the building right behind Daniel. Nobody noticed you, because we thought we'd already found a close-up of the killer." He paused for a moment, studying her. Her jaw was tense. She seemed impatient to see where he was going with this. "That was, until I read your blog. In French, your father's native language. That's when I realized I should be looking for someone else in that video." He said this all in a rush, then went silent.

He thought that the fact he'd discovered her blog would surprise her, but her reaction was unexpected. Adele seemed to relax, and smiled. She no longer seemed upset at all; in fact she looked relieved.

Eric understood at once. "You wanted me to find it?" he murmured. "Of course you did," he added, answering his own question. "Otherwise why leave it up online all this time?"

"How did you recognize me in the video?" She was clearly calmer now, with no obvious signs of preoccupation.

Her question diverted Eric from the line of reasoning he'd been following. "The tattoo on your wrist. You forgot to cover it up."

She raised the hand holding the gun and looked at the lotus flower tattooed on her left wrist. It seemed to amuse her. "What an idiot!" she said.

Shaw didn't know how he should interpret her behavior. She knew she'd been discovered and seemed ready to confess everything. She didn't have anything left to lose, but she still had a gun in her hand. And Eric, the only one who had figured out her secret and had the evidence to prove it, was right there with her, alone. This woman had killed three people, four if you counted Dillon. She'd been there when Garnish died. There was no doubt in his mind that she hadn't lifted a finger to help him. What difference would one more murder make?

He'd made a serious mistake, confronting her like this without taking any precautions. Once again he'd been ingenuous when it came to Adele. He glanced at the door. He was fewer than six yards away from safety, but he'd be an easy target on his way there. He'd gone into her house without knocking in the middle of the night, and she'd thought he was a thief breaking in. She could easily claim she'd shot him a fraction of a second before realizing it was her boyfriend. She would probably get away with it.

Eric knew he was a dead man. This knowledge must have been clear on his face, because Adele laughed mockingly. He had to play for time, get her to talk, distract her somehow. He had to get close to her and take her gun away.

"Your plan really was perfect," said Eric, showing as much admiration as he could possibly muster. "You got the investigators to believe the killer was a man for the first murder. You got that little boy, Sayyid, to notice the figure in black when he hadn't even noticed you. Who knows how many couriers walk in and out of that building every day?" Eric said, attempting to compliment her intelligence. His ploy appeared to be working—Adele was clearly pleased to hear him say it. "But I still can't figure out exactly how it happened. Did you kill him together?"

Adele licked her lips before speaking. "No," she murmured, shaking her head slightly. "I went in first and killed him." She was calm, as if killing a man were an everyday affair. "Danny waited on the stairs. I sent him a message, and then he came into Thompson's apartment. He helped me get rid of all the evidence. I hid it in the package I'd brought with me." She smiled for a moment, apparently particularly proud of the way she'd managed the whole situation. "Then we waited until we heard movement in the hallway. I'd been watching that building for a long time. I knew there were people walking in and out of it day and night."

"You wanted to make sure someone saw a woman in black walk out of that apartment," Eric said with a nod.

"That's right." She nodded. "We heard the little boy playing in the hallway. Danny stuck his head out the door to look, and when he saw the boy turn the other way, he motioned for me to leave. I stopped and waited on the landing while Danny closed the door, making sure he made enough noise to attract Sayyid's attention and ensure that the boy would see him." She tilted her head to one side and examined an invisible spot somewhere on the wall. "Then we left," she finished, not the least bit concerned that she'd just confessed to murder.

"So you waited until the murder was discovered before you committed the second murder, taking advantage of the figure in black again so that we would make an immediate connection between the two and keep focusing on an imaginary male assassin dressed in bizarre clothing." Eric chuckled, feigning amusement. "Genius. Except it was you dressed in black for the second murder, wasn't it?" His hilarity faded as he remembered the arm lifting up, the aiming and shooting he'd seen in the other surveillance video. The left hand. The killer was left-handed. "Of course it was you." He hadn't missed that detail, but somehow it had gotten lost in the course of events. Now Adele's left hand was holding her police pistol. He'd seen her use that hand countless times—to write, to make a gesture, to caress his face—and yet he'd never made the connection before. No. That wasn't right. He hadn't *wanted* to make the connection.

"I kept Danny out of the other murders. I didn't want to get him any more involved than was absolutely necessary."

"That was sweet of you." Shaw couldn't hide his sarcasm, but it didn't appear to bother Adele all that much. "After you killed the other two, you exchanged your pistol for Garnish's nine-millimeter in the car, but you couldn't have known he'd use that gun to kill Daniel."

Adele's face contorted.

Eric didn't let himself be intimidated. "Garnish had already figured out you were behind those murders. He's the one who attacked you outside Jane's party, wasn't he?"

Tears began to run down the woman's face, but she didn't answer him. She didn't need to.

"He must have guessed Daniel was helping you. During the interrogation, he thought we were trying to frame him. But"—Eric raised his voice—"you should have known he would come to look for you at home, at your old address. But you didn't think of it. And now Danny's dead." This time, he used her ex-husband's nickname on purpose. "Dead because of you."

"Shut up!" shouted Adele, raising the pistol and pointing it at him.

Eric raised his hands as if he were giving up. He knew it was a risk, but he had to force her to acknowledge her responsibility. Maybe he could confuse her enough that he'd be able to take control of the situation. "It's the truth and you know it." His tone was aggressive now. "You can murder me, right here and now, but that won't bring Danny back to life. It won't change the fact that if only you hadn't been so egotistical, if only you had thought of something other than your own personal vendetta, Danny would still be alive right now."

"I *had* to!" she shouted, still keeping her gun trained on Eric. "*You* and your colleagues didn't do a thing! My family died, and you couldn't even figure out who killed them! And you had them right in your hands!" Her rage seemed overpowering, uncontrollable. "I saw all four of them, but I was only seven years old. Ah! You didn't even dream of asking me what I'd seen. That goddamned crackpot shrink . . ." Adele kept turning the gun this way and that as she spoke. "He told you all that I was in shock, that it didn't make any sense to interrogate me, and you were all too happy to let him have his way."

"I didn't conduct the investigation!" protested Eric, shouting back. He took a small step toward her. "I was the last person to join that team. I couldn't make any decisions. All I did was catalogue evidence and conduct analyses. It certainly wasn't my fault Garnish slipped through our fingers!"

Adele seemed to calm down again. "I know," she said, her voice little more than a whisper. "I was never angry at you. You saved me." She smiled through her tears. "Garnish and his gang killed me along with the rest of my family. You created a new me."

He could see the very real gratitude on the woman's face. For the first time, Eric began to think that she didn't actually mean to kill him.

"Thanks to you I became a criminologist," she continued. "I wanted to join the police force, to hunt down the men who'd killed my parents and nail them. I wanted them to pay for their crimes. I wanted to send them all to jail. That was the revenge, the vendetta I wanted."

Shaw was listening. Was she serious, or was she still trying to manipulate him? She seemed so sincere . . .

"But I reexamined the entire case, all the evidence. I didn't find any proof. It was just my word, the word of a little seven-year-old girl who'd waited almost twenty years to say her piece. Then, when I started working with you, I saw how things really work."

He could see where she was going with this, and a sense of dread rose inside of him.

"I saw the things you did to make sure criminals got justice. That's when I understood there was another way to achieve my goals. It was too late to make up some fake evidence, but I could still make sure those bastards got what was coming to them."

"No . . . ," whispered Eric, shaking his head. He couldn't believe what he was hearing.

"You are my mentor," said Adele. Her tone was affectionate. "When you carried me out of that house, I was reborn. You created me. And everything I know, I've learned from you over these years. I kept an eye on you, because I considered you a member of my family. I followed your career, one success after another. I wanted to be like you, to fight criminals by your side. And I did."

Eric felt utterly powerless. He knew he should argue, but he didn't know what to say. He couldn't let her compare the things she'd done to the unorthodox ways he'd managed to pin guilt on some criminals. He couldn't accept that she somehow considered him responsible for what she'd become.

"But I wasn't supposed to fall in love with you." Her voice turned hesitant. "I wasn't. But I did."

"*No!* I won't let you do it!" exclaimed Eric suddenly. "I won't let you put us both on the same level! I've twisted some evidence a little in order to send criminals I *knew* were guilty to prison. I did it because the system often fails us. I've never killed anyone! I would never dream of killing somebody!"

"That's just because you've never been a victim," responded Adele, keeping her composure. "If you'd gone through what I experienced, you wouldn't judge what I've done the same way."

Of course. How could he know? He'd never seen his own family killed before his very eyes, yet he couldn't, wouldn't justify the way she'd brought them to justice. It went against everything he believed in.

At the same time, he remembered the pleasure he'd felt shooting Garnish. The memory of that pleasure crawled across his mind, throwing all his certainties into doubt.

"My father gave his life for me," continued Adele. She was still holding the gun, but she seemed less convinced now. "He had to be vindicated."

"What do you mean?" he asked. Her father hadn't told the killers where the safe was kept. He had chosen to die, leaving his daughter a considerable inheritance. Was that what she meant? Something didn't add up.

"The safe was in my room, in the attic. No one thought to look up there. They didn't even know I existed. Garnish knew about the jewelry, but he didn't even bother figuring out how many members of the family there were."

"Oh my God," murmured Eric. Suddenly everything was clear.

"My father let himself be tortured to death because he realized they didn't know about me. If he'd told them where the safe was, they would have discovered my room and searched the house for me. They would have found me, and they would have killed me. Just like they did with everyone else. Do you understand?" Tears were flowing freely down her face now. "I heard his screams. I heard all their screams. I kept my hands pressed against my ears." She mimicked the position she'd held, pressing her hands and even the pistol against her head. "But they were so loud I could still hear them. I didn't think they would ever stop." Adele was weeping openly, hiccupping and shaking, but the grip on her gun never wavered, even with her arms wrapped around her torso now.

Eric was struggling. Part of him wanted to hug her close, reassure her, tell her that everything was going to be all right. In spite of everything, Adele was still the woman he loved, but that didn't change what she'd done. He didn't know if he could ever truly forgive her, even though he knew she was the person most in need of his help. If she wound up in prison, it wouldn't make a difference. She wasn't dangerous anymore. She'd completed her vendetta, and maybe she didn't have much of anything else left. Except for him.

They stood there for a few minutes, she crying silently and he thinking, uncertain what to do next.

Then Adele began to calm down. She dried the tears from her face with her free hand and stared back at him. She seemed to have exhausted all her energies. He could find no trace of emotion left in her. No anger, no love, not even pain. It was like looking at a ghost.

"I did what I had to do," said Adele. "My parents, Paul, and Danny . . . finally they can all rest in peace." Her tone was neutral, like listening to an automaton. Then a faint spark flared briefly in her eyes. "I'm only sorry it means I'll lose you."

I tried to read the thoughts behind his gaze. At first he was going to arrest me, I'm sure of it. He was worried I might shoot him, otherwise he would have. But then his attitude changed, once he realized I had absolutely no intention of harming him. He didn't want me to suffer any more than I already have over all these long years. How could he? He loves me. I know it.

I did everything I could to make him love me, because I love him. I always have. Ever since I looked into his eyes in the garden outside my parents' house, from that very moment I knew that he was my future. They say a seven-year-old is too young to understand certain things, but I knew right then and there that I wanted this man to love me.

I spent a lifetime watching him, observing him, learning everything I could about him, about his family, about his son.

When I learned he had gotten separated, I knew the time had come to move a little closer to him. It took me time to finish my studies in criminology and to get hired onto his team, but I pulled it off in the end. And ever since then I've concentrated all my strength and all my efforts on making sure the thought of me worked its way into his head.

In a certain sense it was fun. It was all a question of doing the right thing at the right moment, like when I slipped a tranquillizer into his beer that night in the pub and brought him home to sleep in my apartment. He was lying there, knocked out, defenseless, completely in my power. My darling Eric.

In the end I did it. I got him to love me. And now he's about to abandon his principles for me.

But there was something else I knew: it would be difficult, practically impossible, for him to forgive me. And without him, my life wouldn't make sense anymore.

I kept the blog online, ticking like a time bomb. Eric spoke a little French and would be able to understand its content. I couldn't carry that weight around forever. I had to share it with him one way or another. I just didn't have the courage to confess to him face to face.

So I decided to leave my destiny to chance. If he discovered the blog, it would mean my time was up.

It was short, but sweet, and I've enjoyed every minute of it. There's just one thing left to do . . .

Adele tightened her grip on the pistol and brought the barrel up under her chin.

Eric felt terror seize his heart. Time seemed to stand still, his eyes fixed on Adele's index finger trembling on the trigger, flexing, starting to pull back.

Driven by an irrational impulse, his body launched out toward her. He no longer cared about his own life as he reached out with both hands to grab Adele's left wrist.

The roar of the bullet exploding filled the room. The mirror hanging on the wall shattered into a thousand pieces, launching shards in all directions. Eric and Adele fell down on their knees together. His hands were holding her arm to one side, the gun slipping out of her fingers and onto the floor. They stared into each other's eyes for a long time.

Adele was the first to break the silence. "It's over between us, isn't it?" she said.

Eric was asking himself the same thing.

At last he nodded, but he didn't know if it really was. Maybe it was just the beginning.

ACKNOWLEDGMENTS

I would like to thank the members of my editorial team, all of whom helped bring this book to life: Gabriella Serrenti, Alberto Casu, Alessandra Fadda, Stefania Mattana, Silvia Marongiu, Silvia Molinari, Giorgio Guerreri, Maristella Di Caprio, Andrea Bisognin, and Marco Mincarini.

Special thanks go to Veronica DeLorenzo, who provided extensive comments for the first draft of the novel; to my parents, who have learned to love every literary genre I've tackled; and especially to Federico Fadda, my number-one fan and test reader par excellence, for his unwavering love and support.

I would also like to thank all the readers who followed my Red Desert series and decided to try this book as well, even though it isn't science fiction. I hope you enjoyed the read!

ABOUT THE AUTHOR

Rita Carla Francesca Monticelli was born in Carbonia, Italy. She has lived in Cagliari since 1993, earning a degree in biology and working as a writer, researcher, scientific and literary translator, and freelance web copywriter. Monticelli has authored *L'isola di Gaia* (*The Isle of Gaia*), *Affinità d'intenti* (*Kindred Intentions*), and the science fiction series Deserto rosso (Red Desert), which is also available in English. *The Mentor* is her sixth book.

ABOUT THE TRANSLATOR

Photo © 2012 Davide Carlesso

Aaron Maines is a freelance writer and literary translator based in Milan, Italy. He has written for a number of publications on both sides of the Atlantic, including the *Wall Street Journal*, the *Washington Post*, and the *New York Times* in the United States, as well as *Cartier Art* and *L'Europeo* in Europe.

Maines has translated books and essays by Umberto Eco, Oriana Fallaci, Elisabetta Dami (Geronimo Stilton), Tullio Kezich, Andrea De Carlo, and others. In 2007, he was chosen to translate filmmaker Federico Fellini's personal diary, *The Book of Dreams*.